## Praise for Kate Hoffmann
## from *RT Book Reviews*

### The Charmer
"Hoffmann's deeply felt, emotional story
is riveting. It's impossible to put down."

### Your Bed or Mine?
"Fully developed characters and perfect pacing
make this story feel completely right."

### Doing Ireland!
"Sexy and wildly romantic."

### The Mighty Quinns: Ian
"A very hot story mixes with great characters
to make every page a delight."

### Who Needs Mistletoe?
"Romantic, sexy and heartwarming."

### The Mighty Quinns: Teague
"Sexy, heartwarming and romantic...a story
to settle down with and enjoy—and then re-read."

Dear Reader,

Another Quinn trilogy is coming to a close and this one has been a lot of fun to write, especially since it took me back to one of my favorite places, Ireland.

Though I've only been to Ireland once, I've spent the last year thinking about all the wonderful and picturesque towns I visited. Someday, I hope to return for another visit, maybe even during the holidays. I could even search out my one lonely Irish ancestor. I'd drive past the spot on the coast where Ballykirk should be and wander down the country road where Winterhill might have stood. And if I'm lucky, I might even meet a man who looks a little bit like Kellan Quinn. You couldn't ask for a better Christmas present than that.

If you've never had a chance to visit the Emerald Isle, I hope this Quinn trilogy has given you a little taste of one of my favorite places.

Happy holidays,

Kate Hoffmann

# Kate Hoffmann

## THE MIGHTY QUINNS: KELLAN

TORONTO NEW YORK LONDON
AMSTERDAM PARIS SYDNEY HAMBURG
STOCKHOLM ATHENS TOKYO MILAN MADRID
PRAGUE WARSAW BUDAPEST AUCKLAND

Recycling programs
for this product may
not exist in your area.

ISBN-13: 978-0-373-79657-1

THE MIGHTY QUINNS: KELLAN

www.Harlequin.com

**Printed in U.S.A.**

## ABOUT THE AUTHOR

Kate Hoffmann began writing for Harlequin Books in 1993. Since then she's published sixty-five books, primarily in the Harlequin Temptation and Harlequin Blaze lines. When she isn't writing, she enjoys music, theater and musical theater. She is active working with high school students in the performing arts. She lives in southeastern Wisconsin with her cat, Chloe.

### Books by Kate Hoffmann

# *Prologue*

KELLAN STARED out at the water from the narrow beach, the morning sun gleamed off the glassy surface of the Atlantic. He drew a deep breath and smiled. It was the perfect summer day. Warm without a hint of the damp wind that usually roared along the coast.

"We should sleep here tonight," he said to his brothers. "Up on the cliff. Da would let us take the tent." Glancing over his shoulder, he found Riley and Danny squatting down and digging in the sand.

Smuggler's Cove had become their secret getaway. Just five or six kilometers from their cottage outside Ballykirk, the hidden cove could only be reached from the water. But Danny, Kellan's youngest brother, had discovered a path down through the rocks, making the spot accessible.

"I'm not spendin' the night," Riley said. "There's ghosts in that old house up there." He was talking about the abandoned castle and manor house that overlooked the cliff. None of them had ever been brave enough to venture inside, although Kellan had heard the older kids used the place for parties all the time.

"Me, neither," Danny said.

"What the feck are you two about?" Kellan asked, watching as they scraped sand aside with their fingers.

"There's something buried in the sand," Danny said, burrowing after it like a terrier after a bone. "Come here and help, ya lazy git."

"No way. You've been digging in that sand for two years now and you haven't found a thing. Considering the smugglers are long gone, it's probably just an old piece of wood. You and your fantasies. They're a waste of time."

Riley stopped for a moment. "If Kell doesn't dig and it is treasure, then he doesn't get a share."

"Agreed," Danny said.

"Yeah," Kellan said. "Agreed." But to Kellan's surprise, Danny and Riley pulled a small tin box out of the sand. "What the feck," he muttered, striding over to them.

"See," Danny said smugly. "Told you. Now you don't get a share." He brushed the sand off the top of the old biscuit tin.

"Open it," Riley urged.

Danny reached for the top, then hesitated. "I don't know. What if it's cursed? It could be like…like…"

"Pandora's box," Kellan told him. "Jaysus, you two are always letting your imagination run away with you. It's a feckin' biscuit tin."

"Should we open it?" Danny asked, looking to

Kellan for an answer. They always looked to him for answers. That's what it was to be the oldest boy in the Quinn family.

Kellan shrugged. "You found it. You open it." He turned away, determined not to show his interest. But as he did, he caught sight of a movement among the rocks on the cliffside. He stared at the spot for a long moment, then shook his head. But there it was again. A flutter of pale green fabric in the breeze and a slender form scrambling behind another rock.

"There's someone up there," he muttered. "Watching us."

The boys looked up from their examination of the box, following Kellan's nod. "Right up there."

"Maybe it's a fairy," Riley said. "And maybe this is her box of magic. Let's go see if we can catch her." Riley shoved the box at Danny and leaped to his feet, then took off for the path at the bottom of the rocks.

"Wait," Danny called. "What if it's a ghost from the house?"

Kellan heard a tiny cry from above him and he watched the girl scamper along the path, climbing up and over the rocks. She looked like a fairy, her long, golden hair draped over her back and crowned by a wreath of wildflowers. But she didn't have wings, at least none that he could see. She was dressed in an old gown made of a sheer fabric so light it floated around her.

Cursing to himself, Kellan followed his brothers. What was he thinking? He knew fairies weren't real.

Maybe his little brothers believed, but Kellan was far too pragmatic to put any faith in Irish myths and legends. "Leave me to it," he said, hurrying past Riley. "I can climb faster than you."

Kellan scrambled up the path, but each time he looked for her, she was putting more distance between them. If she really were a fairy, she'd just fly away. No, this was a girl, a girl he'd never seen before. Kellan knew all the girls living around Ballykirk and not one of them was half as beautiful as this one.

Breathless, he reached the top of the cliff only to find her halfway across the meadow. She turned once and laughed, then took her crown of wildflowers and threw it into the air.

"Wait!" Kellan called. "Don't go. I want to talk to you."

She spun around and stood, staring at him, waiting as he ran toward her. When he reached her, Kellan stopped, his heart pounding, gasping for breath. She *was* the most beautiful thing he'd ever seen, features so perfect that they couldn't belong to anything human.

"Open the box," she said, the musical tone of her voice ringing in the still summer air. "I put it there for you."

Kellan heard his brothers behind him, calling his name. "Who are you?"

With a laugh, she came closer and dropped a kiss on his lips. "I'm a dream," she said. "Close your eyes and I'll disappear."

Kellan glanced back to see his brothers quickly approaching, but when he turned to the girl again, she had already run from him. This time, Kellan decided not to follow.

"You're letting her get away," Danny called. "Go after her, Kellan."

"She's not a fairy," Kellan said when Danny and Riley reached him. He touched his lips, still warm from her kiss. "She's just a girl. A silly old girl."

They watched her retreat together, then Kellan grabbed the tin from beneath Riley's arm. "Let's see what's inside."

"I thought Danny said it might be cursed."

"Do you believe everything he says?" Kellan asked. "Riley, sometimes you're as thick as a post."

He tugged off the top and peered inside. The tin was filled with a variety of items—a seashell, a few pretty stones, a necklace made of flowers, braided string.

"Aw, it's nothing but junk," Riley said.

Danny swore. "I was hoping it might at least be worth a few quid."

"I think we should bury it again," Kellan said. If they did, she might come back for it. He could hide in the rocks and watch for her. Catching a fairy was powerful luck, wasn't it?

"I'm not climbing back down." Danny started off toward home. "I'm hungry. And Ma will have lunch for us soon."

Riley followed him, a dejected look on his face. "I thought it would be treasure. I thought we'd be rich."

Kellan sighed softly, then plopped down onto the

grass. Crossing his legs in front of him, he reopened the tin and carefully picked through the contents. There were jeweled buttons and a penny whistle, a scrap of lace and three pieces of butterscotch candy. Why the girl had decided to bury it in the sand, he didn't know. But he couldn't help but be intrigued.

Who was she? Would she return to the cove or was she really a visitor from another world? For the first time in his life, Kellan felt an odd attraction, a strange fascination with a girl.

Would he ever understand the opposite sex? The girls in school were annoying. Though they were constantly following him about, whispering and giggling, they were all uninteresting to his eyes. And his two older sisters, Shanna and Claire, were a complete mystery and a royal pain in his arse. But this...this lovely creature was magical. He closed his eyes and lay in the grass, letting his imagination wander, back to the kiss she'd given him.

He'd never kissed a girl. He was nearly fifteen years old and though most of his friends had enjoyed the experience at least once or twice, Kellan had never taken advantage of his opportunities, until now.

He grinned. If he ever saw the fairy girl again, he'd do it even better. He'd grab her and kiss her, right on the lips, and see what she had to say about that. Now that he knew exactly what he wanted in a girl, what he'd been looking for, everything made sense.

She had to be...extraordinary. He'd settle for nothing less. Someday soon, maybe she'd come back to the cove, looking for her tin of treasures. He'd find a proper place to hide it until then.

# *1*

THE WEATHER WAS unusually warm for late November. Kellan Quinn stared out at the sea from his spot above Smuggler's Cove. He walked over to the rocky edge of the cliff to look down at the narrow strip of beach where he and his brothers used to play. He hadn't been down the path in years, not since before he left for university.

But the little beach, sheltered from the wind, would be a perfect place to think, to find some solitude and clear his head. Life in Ballykirk had turned into a whirl of activity since his younger brothers had both found mates, and though he was happy for them, lately he'd felt like the odd man out.

Riley would be getting married in just over a month and though he and Nan had planned a simple New Year's Eve ceremony at the village church and a reception at the pub, it promised to be the biggest social event Ballykirk had seen in quite some time. Both Danny and Kellan would be standing up with Riley, which didn't sound like much. However, Kellan had learned that serving as a groomsman meant that you were at the beck and call of the groom until he left for his honeymoon.

Kellan still couldn't get over how quickly things had changed for the Quinn brothers. Riley and Danny had both fallen for American girls in the space of a few months. Of course, everyone assumed Kellan would be next and to that end, they'd started to put interested single girls in his path. But he knew better.

When it came to romance, Kellan Quinn was a realist. The chances of finding lasting love were slim at best. Though he'd turned thirty last year, he really hadn't ever come close to marriage, or enjoyed a long-term relationship. Perhaps it was because he'd never found a woman who could hold his attention. A woman who was more interesting than his career.

His reputation as an architect was growing with every project he completed and he was usually at the top of the list for any major historical renovation in Ireland. Though it wasn't really cutting-edge architecture, Kellan enjoyed doing his part to preserve pieces of Ireland's past.

Sixteen-hour days didn't leave much time for a social life, but he did manage to date occasionally when he stayed at his flat in Dublin. There were women who were happy to have him warm their bed, no strings, no expectations. But the relationships lacked an emotional component, existing purely for physical release.

Kellan drew a deep breath of the damp air. Riley

and Danny had found their perfect matches. It was as if both women had just dropped out of the sky and into their beds. Had they been searching, waiting, wondering?

The wind buffeted his body and Kellan pulled his canvas jacket closed. In the past few days, a strange restlessness had come over him. Something was about to change. He could feel it inside, like the sky darkening before a storm.

He'd had an offer to do a project in France and he'd been considering the opportunity. It would mean moving to Brittany for a year to supervise the renovation of an old armory into a World War II museum. Maybe it was time for a change. Maybe he needed something new in his life...just like his brothers.

Raking his hands through his windblown hair, Kellan walked to the rocks and searched for the way down. The descent was easy once he found the right path. As he clambered over the jagged traverse, he noticed something odd lying on the beach.

At first, it looked like a pile of debris and seaweed. But as he got closer, his heart started to pound. It was a body! He made out a long, slender arm and the unmistakable curve of a woman's hip. Kellan jumped down the last five feet and ran over to her, almost dreading what he was about to discover.

But the moment he touched her, she jerked, then sat up, brushing the damp strands of hair from her eyes. She looked at him through eyes so pale they were almost colorless.

"Are you all right?"

A tiny frown worried her brow, but she made no attempt to speak.

"What are you doing down here? How did you get here? Were you in the water?"

She reached out and smoothed her sand-covered palm over his cheek, her gaze studying the details of his face. And then, without warning, she leaned forward and touched her lips to his. She tasted of salt water and smelled of the ocean breeze.

The kiss was so surprising, he jerked back. But she was determined and slipped her hand around his nape, pulling him closer, drawing him down into the sand with her. Kellan normally exercised a great deal of self-restraint around women. But the moment her lips touched his, his control dissolved into an overwhelming need.

Her lips parted on a sigh and he took the chance to taste, his tongue delving into the sweet warmth of her mouth. She responded immediately, writhing beneath him as if trying to get closer. Her body trembled and when he finally drew back he realized it wasn't from the impact of their kiss but from the cold.

"Are you all right?" he asked again. "What's your name?"

Her eyes fluttered and then closed as she went limp in his arms. Kellan grabbed her chin and turned her head. She was still breathing, but just barely. Cursing, he scrambled to his feet and picked her up, hoping that she'd regain consciousness. She was dead weight in his arms, like a rag doll.

Kellan looked up to the top of the cliff. The only way to get her up was tossed over his shoulder. It wouldn't be comfortable, but there was no other option.

The dress she wore was barely enough to keep her warm in midsummer much less late autumn. Just a thin layer of green silk. He shrugged out of his canvas jacket and struggled to get her into it, buttoning it up once he had. "I don't know who the hell you are, but you should count yourself bloody lucky I came along."

He bent down and grabbed her thighs, her body folding over his shoulder. The path was narrow but navigable, even with a passenger. He had to be cautious of her head, careful not to bump her against the rocks. When he finally reached the top, Kellan set her down in the grass and took a deep breath.

Her eyes fluttered again and for a moment she opened them. "Can you stand up?" he asked.

Her lips curled into a sleepy smile and she shook her head and closed her eyes again.

"What the hell am I supposed to do with you?" he muttered. "If the hike home doesn't kill you, it will probably kill me."

He couldn't leave her here alone. But he could probably run home and fetch his car in less time than it would take to carry her. The hike to the road was only about half a kilometer. Home was nearly five.

He had his mobile. He'd ring the pub and see if one of his brothers could drive out. Meanwhile, he'd try to get her warm and awake. He flipped open his phone and to his relief, Danny answered almost immediately.

"I need your help," Kellan said. "I need you to drive up the coast road and park your car just around the bend by the dry stone fence, before you get to Castle Cnoc. Right where we used to leave our bikes when we'd come down to the cove."

"Why?" Danny asked.

"Just do it. I'll explain when you get here."

"Riley and Nan have me stuffing invitations for their engagement party. This is important stuff I'm workin' on, Kell. I can't just be hopping off for no good reason."

"It's an emergency. Maybe even life or death. Leave now. I'll meet you there in a few minutes."

"I'm on my way."

This time, when Kellan hefted her over his shoulder, she groaned and fought against him. "That's right," he said. "It's not so comfortable, is it? Maybe if you could summon the energy to walk, we might both be spared the trouble of me lugging you through this meadow like a lumpy sack of potatoes."

"Ow," she said.

"What were you doing on that beach, anyway? If I hadn't come along, you'd be on your way to dead right now. Dead and washed away by the tide. That's no way to leave this world. What about your family? They might never have known what happened to you."

"I— Oh, sick," she muttered. A few seconds later, she retched and he felt the back of his leg go damp. After that, she seemed to settle down.

"Lovely. Brilliant." Kellan tried to calm his own stomach. If there was one thing he couldn't handle it was— He felt a wave of nausea overtake him and he stopped and drew a deep breath through his mouth. "I don't know if you're drunk or just crazy, but you'll be thanking me for this later."

By the time he reached the road, Danny was waiting in his battered old Land Rover. His brother jumped out of the driver's side and ran up to him. "What the devil! Where did you find her?"

"On the beach at the cove. She's cold and I think she might be drunk. Or sick. I don't know."

"What are you going to do with her?"

"Take her back to the cottage. I'll get her warm and call Doc Finnerty."

"Maybe we should drive her directly to the hospital?"

"All the way to Cork? Let's get her out of these wet clothes first and warm her up. If she doesn't come round, I'll take her."

When they got her settled in the backseat, Kellan slid in beside her, resting her head on his lap. Danny turned the car around and raced back toward town. At the fork in the road, he turned up toward the cottage.

Kellan had been living in Ballykirk for the past couple weeks, taking a break from life in Dublin while his family planned for the upcoming wedding. The small, whitewashed cottage had been his childhood home, set on a high rise above the seaside village. On occasion, it was let out to tourists, but when it wasn't, Kellan often stayed there.

When Danny pulled the car to a stop, Kellan got out and carefully scooped the woman up into his arms. "Do me a favor. Give Doc Finnerty a call and if he doesn't answer, see if you can find him."

"I know where he is," Danny said. "He's having a pint at the pub. He was there when I left." He ran up the garden path and opened the door for Kellan. "I'll go get him, then."

Kellan turned toward the bedroom, then realized that the sofa was a better choice. He could light a fire and it would provide the warmth she needed. He set her down, then hurriedly laid peat and kindling in the hearth. A few minutes later, a flicker of flame licked at the sod, smoke curling up into the chimney.

"There," he said. He leaned back on his heels, then realized the fire would do only half the job. He had to get her out of her wet clothes and into something warm. Though he didn't relish undressing a woman without her permission, Kellan figured if he didn't look at her in a sexual way, it would remain a purely practical matter.

He strode into the bedroom and grabbed the quilt and a wool blanket off the bed, then returned to the sofa. She was so still, curled up in front of him. Kellan gently sat her up, then slipped his jacket off her shoulders.

If she were conscious, he could put her in a warm shower. But there was no way she could stand unless he joined her.

Her hair was tangled with sand and bits of debris from the beach. He managed to skim her damp dress up along her legs, but was forced to pull her to her feet to get it over her head. To his relief, she seemed able to stand on her own for a few seconds.

He tossed the dress aside, then grabbed the quilt, wrapping her up in it and trying not to dwell on the fact that she wasn't wearing any underwear. "Why should that surprise me?" he murmured.

She had a beautiful body, slender and long-limbed. Her skin was pale and soft as silk, but so cold to his touch. His gaze slipped lower, to her lovely breasts, the curve of her hips and the junction of her legs.

He drew a ragged breath and pulled her against him, rubbing her back with his palms until the friction created warmth. What she really needed was a long, hot bath. But the cottage had only a shower. A bath would require hauling in the old tub that they'd used as kids.

A sharp knock sounded on the door and a few seconds later, Danny stepped inside followed by Jimmy Finnerty. Dr. Finnerty was the closest thing the town had to a local doctor. He had retired from his practice in Cork three years ago and now lived a quiet life with his wife in his vacation home on the bay, spending his days fishing and only coming out of retirement for the occasional emergency.

"What have we here?" he asked, setting his bag on the end of the sofa.

"I found her on the beach," Kellan said.

"The beach? What beach?"

"A little spot I know just up the coast. She was lying in the sand."

"Naked?"

"No, she was dressed. I took her dress off to try to get her warm. I think she's a bit better. I had her standing. But she hasn't really opened her eyes."

The doctor reached into his bag and pulled out a small vial, then cracked it and held the smelling salts under her nose. She jerked back, then waved her hand in front of her face, moaning softly. "Well, she's not unconscious. She seems to be under the influence."

"Of what?" Danny asked.

"Pills. Liquor. Can't say for certain. Why don't we start with some nice hot coffee and see if that helps." He glanced over at Kellan. "You say you found her on the beach?"

Kellan nodded. "She threw up while I was carrying her out to the road."

"That's a positive sign."

"Not for me," he muttered.

"You don't suppose she's a—"

"A drunk?"

"No, a mermaid," Finnerty said with a chuckle. "She could be a mermaid washed up onshore."

"Look at her," Danny said. "She has that look about her."

Kellan stared at the woman, frowning. "She looks… I don't know. Pretty. But she has feet. Don't mermaids have…fins?"

"Naw. Not after they come ashore," Finnerty said

as he slipped on a blood pressure cuff. "The skin is so pale and the hair like spun silk. I've seen pictures. This is what they look like. Otherworldly. Was she combing her hair when you first saw her?" He looked up. "That's how they cast their spells, you know."

"I don't believe in mermaids," Kellan said. "And neither do you two. She was unconscious when I found her."

Finnerty listened to her pulse, then removed the cuff. "Well, she's here. And her vital signs are strong. What are you going to do with her?"

"I thought you could take her. To hospital, if need be."

"She appears to be slightly hypothermic and possibly hungover. Now that she's getting warm, she'll probably wake up and be just fine. I expect the best place for her is right here—at least until she's feeling better. Then you can take her back where you found her."

"What? I can't put her back on that beach."

"Well, I'm sure you'll sort it all out," Finnerty said as he rose from the sofa. "You're a smart lad, Kellan. Now, my wife has dinner waiting and I'm late. If you need me, give me a ring and I'll come back. Danny, let's be off and leave your brother to nurse this pretty merrow back to health."

Danny gave Kellan a shrug and followed the doctor out the door. "Bring me up some soup from the pub," Kellan called. "And a bottle of whiskey."

"No problem," Danny said. "And I'll fetch a bushel

of kelp and some herring, too." He was still chuckling as the door slammed behind him.

Kellan stared down at the woman lying on the sofa. He reached down and brushed the flaxen hair from her eyes, taking in the perfect features of her face. Finnerty was right. She had a look about her, something…extraordinary. "Otherworldly," he murmured.

And familiar. Kellan couldn't shake the feeling that he'd seen her somewhere before. And yet, he certainly would have remembered meeting her. A woman this beautiful would have stuck in his mind.

"If you are a mermaid," he murmured, smoothing his hand over her temple, "then we're going to have a very interesting conversation when you wake up."

GELSEY WOODSON SNUGGLED into the warm recesses of the blanket wrapped around her naked body. Her head ached from the bottle of champagne she'd drunk the night before and her skin itched from salt water and sand, but she couldn't bring herself to open her eyes.

She listened distractedly to the male voices, realizing they were talking about her. The one man was obviously a doctor and she stifled a moan as he took her blood pressure. There was another voice, her rescuer. The man who'd carried her up from the beach. She liked his voice. It was like liquid chocolate, smooth and dark and just a bit sweet.

Their conversation turned to mermaids and for a moment she was confused, until she realized that they thought she was a mermaid. That nearly made her laugh out loud. She'd always been one to indulge in fantasies. From the time she was a child, she'd woven a rich imaginary life for herself where she was a princess one day and a fairy queen the next, or a sorceress or an elf or a pixie with powers that could change her world in the blink of an eye.

And now she was a mermaid. Maybe that was for the best, she mused. For she certainly didn't want to be Gelsey Woodson anymore.

Her stomach growled and she winced, remembering the humiliation of vomiting over the man's shoulder. Though she was used to overindulging, bouncing around as he carried her had been a recipe for disaster.

She pulled the blanket up more tightly around her nose. Just a few more hours of rest would be enough. Then she could face the world again. But even though she wanted to sleep, she couldn't help but be curious about the man who'd plucked her off the beach.

When the house went quiet, she slowly opened her eyes and looked around. A fire flickered on the hearth and the acrid smell of peat teased at her nose. She glanced under the quilt. Though she was certain she hadn't undressed herself, she couldn't remember who had.

Her mind wandered back to the previous night. Though she'd done her share of stupid things, especially when it came to her relationships with men, this might just top the list. A late-night phone call, an argument with her ex-fiancé and too much to drink had ended with her tossing a nine carat diamond ring into the sea before passing out on the beach. It seemed as if all her problems had become too heavy to bear. Not just the breakup, but the everything that had come before it—the fights, the paparazzi, the Italian police and the "incident."

That's what she'd taken to calling it. That's what her Italian attorney called it. And that made it sound so benign. But punching a photographer was a serious offense, even if she'd done it while under the influence of another very expensive bottle of champagne and the misunderstanding that the photographer was trying to grope her.

And so she'd run away to Winterhill, to lick her wounds and await her hearing scheduled for late January. Her grandmother's country house in Ireland was a place she'd remembered so fondly from her childhood. The windswept cliffs and brilliant green meadows had been her playground every summer, creating fantasies for a girl used to a solitary existence. She'd come back to find the center in her life again, to hide from everything that confused and frightened her. Though she'd lived all over the world, Ireland had always felt the most like home.

She drew a deep breath and winced, her head throbbing and her mouth dry as dust. Was this what all her therapists had talked about? Everyone had been predicting it. Had Gigi Woodson, tabloid princess and celebrity heiress, finally hit rock bottom?

Her father, Ellery Woodson, was a diplomat for the British government, and her mother, an American socialite. She was their only child and after the first eight years of her life, a pawn in their very nasty divorce. Bad behavior had come easily. It had been the only way to get her parents' attention.

At age twelve, she'd been kicked out of her first boarding school. By seventeen, she'd been kicked out of more schools than she could remember. She had a brief spell of normalcy during her university years in Paris, when she worked on an art history degree and lived with a handsome French banker. But then her grandmother died, leaving her Winterhill and a large trust fund. At age twenty-one, the naughty Gelsey returned with a vengeance—and with a seemingly bottomless bank account.

She'd transformed herself from Gelsey Evangeline Woodson, well-educated daughter of a diplomat, to Gigi Woodson, party girl without a care in the world. For the first five years, it had been fun, like playing make-believe only with posh parties and exciting new friends. Even her mother had approved.

But in the past few years, her life had started to spiral out of control and she began to suspect that she really *did* care. That all the pretending didn't make the loneliness and the insecurities go away. Maybe she hadn't had the best family life and maybe her parents hadn't really wanted her around. But she'd come to realize that the life she was living would never make her happy and the friends she had weren't true friends at all.

Gelsey drew a ragged breath. So, perhaps this could

be a fresh start. Today, this morning. Or afternoon. When she opened her eyes again, she could forget the past and start all over again. She could use what was left of her trust fund and build a simple life for herself, away from the glare of the spotlight and the flash of the paparazzi's cameras.

Her thoughts dissolved and she fell back into a shallow sleep, content for the first time in a long time. Everything would be all right. She'd be safe here, in this tiny cottage. No one knew her in Ireland beyond the housekeeper at Winterhill. No one would care if she stayed away for a day or even a week.

She wasn't sure how long she slept, but the touch of a hand on her face brought her back from a dreamless state of exhaustion. She opened her eyes and found him sitting on the floor near the end of the sofa and staring at her intently.

"You're awake," he murmured.

"Yes," she said, her voice croaking. Gelsey cleared her throat.

"Would you like something warm to drink?" he asked. "I have coffee or tea. Or soup. Or maybe a bit of whiskey?"

Her stomach growled at the mention of food. "Yes, soup would be nice." As for the whiskey, she'd decided to take a new direction in her life. It was time to stop drinking…at least to excess.

"Soup," she said.

"I'll be right back," he murmured.

Gelsey clasped the quilt to her chest as she pulled

herself up to a sitting position. To her surprise, she didn't feel nearly as bad as she'd expected. Just a little bit weak and a tiny bit embarrassed. But she was here, being waited on by a devastatingly handsome man who was making her soup. The first day of her new life was beginning quite well.

As promised, he returned in a few moments with a huge mug and spoon. He sat down beside her and handed her the soup. "It's beef and barley," he said. "It's from the pub down in the village. My ma makes it."

Gelsey took a spoonful. The hearty warmth made her smile. "It's delicious."

"How are you feeling?"

"Fine."

"How is it you came to be on the beach?"

Gelsey opened her mouth to reply, then snapped it shut. She didn't want to explain it all, especially to this man. She didn't want him to think badly of her, to make assumptions and to write her off as some stupid girl without any limits.

"I—I don't know," she said.

"What does that mean?"

Gelsey shrugged. "I don't remember." She took another spoonful of the soup, waiting for him to question her. But he just continued to watch her suspiciously. "I'm not sure."

"Are you saying you have amnesia?"

Gelsey frowned. It sounded like a reasonable diagnosis and it happened all the time in the movies. If she didn't know who she was, then she wouldn't know where she came from. And she could stay here with this man. "I don't know. I just don't remember." She took another spoonful of soup and handed it to him. "I've had enough, thank you."

"You've barely eaten at all," he said.

"What is your name?" she asked.

"Kellan. Kellan Quinn."

A memory flashed in her mind, so clear it might have happened just yesterday. The boy that had chased her from the beach so many years before. His name had been Kellan. She'd heard his brothers yell it across the meadow and she'd committed it to memory. This was the same boy, all grown up.

She smiled to herself. How many times had she woven long and complicated fantasies around that boy? For at least a month after, she'd thought about returning to the beach to find him. But the summer had ended and she'd been sent back to school, leaving thoughts of him far behind.

"Kellan," she repeated. "I like that."

"And what's your name?"

"Gelsey," she replied.

He said it back to her. Softly. The sound of it on his lips caused a shiver to skitter through her body.

"Do you have a last name?" he asked.

"I'm not sure I do," Gelsey said.

A grin teased at the corners of his mouth. "Does that mean you don't remember it or you don't want to tell me what it is?"

"A little of both," she said. She drew in a sharp

breath as her gaze fell to his lips. Lord, he was handsome. She had dated an endless string of gorgeous men, but not one of them had captured her fancy like this man. He was just a regular guy, yet there was something so intriguing about him. "You kissed me," she murmured.

"No," Kellan said.

"You did. I remember. On the beach."

"You kissed me," he said.

"Yes." Gelsey reached out and touched his face, then leaned closer, curious to see if the kiss she remembered was really so good. Her lips found his. He didn't seem surprised or reluctant. Instead, he gently cupped her face in his hands and returned the kiss in full measure, his tongue tangling with hers.

Desire raced through her body, warming her blood and making her mind spin. Gelsey felt giddy, like that breathless young girl on the cliffs. He'd been such a handsome boy, but now he was a man, full grown and capable of making her weak with need.

"Does that help?" he asked.

"Help?"

"Your memory," Kellan said.

"Yes," she said. "I remember liking that very much." She peeked under the blanket. "I have no clothes. Did you undress me?"

Kellan nodded. "You were cold. I had to get you warm."

"I don't remember that." She reached out and took

his hand and placed it on her bare shoulder. "Maybe you should show me how that happened."

Kellan stared at the spot where he touched her, then slowly drew his hand away. "You—you should rest," he murmured. "You've had a long day."

"What time is it?"

"Nearly five," he replied. "Do you have a place to go? Someone who might be waiting for you?"

Gelsey shook her head. "No," she said. "No one is waiting for me." In truth, the only person who'd wonder where she was might be Caroline, the housekeeper at Winterhill. She'd call the first chance she got, but Caroline knew not to worry. Gelsey often disappeared for days at a time.

As for her parents, they'd given up worrying a long time ago. No. No one really cared at all. The only one who'd ever truly cared had been her grandmother and she'd been gone for years now.

"You can stay here until you're feeling better," he said.

"I wouldn't want to put you out," she said.

"You wouldn't be."

"You know what I'd really like? A hot bath. I've got sand in places I didn't even know I had. It feels like I slept in it."

"You did," Kellan said. "I found you on the beach." He stood. "We have a shower. The bathroom is just through the kitchen. Or we have an old tub that I can bring in and fill if you're set on a bath."

"I think a shower would do nicely," Gelsey said. "And I could use some clothes. Do you have my dress?"

"I'll find you something better to wear."

She slowly stood, wrapping the quilt more tightly around her naked body. "Thank you," she said. "For saving me." She paused. "You're a nice man, Kellan. I haven't known too many nice men in my life."

"I'm not all that nice," he replied.

"You can't fool me," she said, pushing up on her toes and placing a kiss on his cheek. Then Gelsey slowly walked toward the bathroom.

As she closed the bathroom door behind her, Gelsey leaned back against it and drew a deep breath. Had he been any other man in her life, she would have seduced him on the spot. She'd never been one to play coy when it came to satisfying her desires. And she'd never met a man who'd refused her.

But that was precisely how she'd gotten into trouble in the past. She'd led with her heart, not her head. Her argument with Antonio last night had been a prime example. She should have been nicer, considering his word would go a long way toward making the assault case disappear. Instead, all the anger and resentment over their breakup had come bubbling to the surface, and after a long predawn phone argument, she'd grabbed a bottle of champagne as the sun came up and wandered along the cliffs to the cove.

Her heart had told her to kiss Kellan that day in the meadow. And her heart had told her to do the same thing when he found her on the beach. And both times, it had felt so right and so real, not wicked or manipulative. Just…perfect.

She didn't have to live her life in brilliant swaths of color and chaos. She could be just like everyone else if she wanted to be—normal. From now on, she'd try to become the kind of woman who didn't indulge her every whim, a woman who controlled her desires and considered her actions.

"Except for kissing," she murmured. After all, what harm could it do to enjoy the lips of a man as handsome and sexy as Kellan Quinn? It was only a matter of time before he found out about her past, about the life she wanted to leave behind. And men like Kellan were not the type to put up with the kind of baggage she carried with her.

Gelsey turned on the shower, then let the quilt drop to the floor. She was warm now, and happy. It was time to take a breath and see life the way everyone else in the world did—without the endless drama and rollercoaster emotions.

# 2

KELLAN SET THE PILE of clothes down next to the bathroom. Though he was trying to keep his mind on other things, it wasn't difficult to imagine what was going on beyond the door. She was naked, obviously. And he'd seen her body when he'd undressed her, so there was no use trying to forget the sweet curves and soft flesh that had been hidden by the quilt.

She'd kissed him not once, but twice. She'd made it quite apparent that she'd welcome more. But Kellan wasn't one to play games when it came to sex and he knew damn well she was hiding something.

She'd refused to provide her last name, which made him suspect she might be running from something or someone—the authorities…or a jealous husband or boyfriend. That was more likely. She didn't seem like the criminal sort. And chances were that a woman as beautiful as Gelsey would have a man in her life. She possessed the kind of beauty that could make any male mad with jealousy.

Kellan cleared his throat, then rapped on the door. "I'm going to run down to the pub and get some supper for us," he called. "I'll be back in about twenty minutes."

"I'm really not very hungry," she replied.

"I am," Kellan said. "Don't make your shower too long. You'll run out of hot water. There are clothes on the floor outside the door."

The bathroom door opened and she poked her head out and smiled. Water droplets clung to her lashes and ran down her cheeks. "Thanks," she said. She bent down and grabbed the clothes and he caught sight of her naked body.

A current of desire raced through him as his gaze settled on a sleek leg, setting his nerves on edge. Kellan couldn't help but look. "Are these yours?" she asked, nodding at the clothes.

"Yes. They won't fit, but they'll keep you warm. For now. I'll see if Nan or Jordan might have something you can borrow."

"Who are Nan and Jordan?"

"Nan is my brother Riley's fiancée and Jordan is my brother Danny's girlfriend."

"I don't mind wearing your clothes," she said.

"But I do." With that, Kellan turned and strode to the door. If she wasn't going to walk around the cottage naked, then at least he'd make sure she had clothes that enhanced her beautiful body.

When he got outside, Kellan took a long deep breath of the cold evening air. The day had begun like any ordinary day, but suddenly, he'd found himself in possession of a beautiful woman, one who planned to spend the night.

A brisk walk into the village should clear his mind of any thoughts of seduction. But he couldn't seem to put Gelsey out of his head. There was something about her, something he found incredibly intriguing.

Kellan made a mental list of all her qualities—the long blond hair, perfectly balanced features, a body that was made to be touched and skin so flawless it made her seem unattainable. But it wasn't just the physical that he found attractive. It was what he didn't know about her that was even more tantalizing.

There was a certain appeal to the idea of a mystery woman, a complete stranger with a secret past. Though he was usually quite rational and fantasies weren't a regular indulgence, Gelsey seemed to bring out the devil in him. What would it be like to have her in his bed, to lose himself inside such a lovely creature?

The pub was busy when he walked in the front door. But the conversation softened to a low murmur the instant everyone saw him enter. He glanced around, then found Danny smiling at him from behind the bar. "There he is!" Danny shouted. "The hero of the day. So what did you do with your mermaid, Kell? Did ya toss her back? Or have you decided to keep her?"

Kellan cursed beneath his breath. No doubt everyone in town was aware of the situation unfolding at the cottage. Maybe that was for the best. Someone in town must know who she was or where she came from.

"She's not a mermaid," he shouted, crossing the room to the bar.

"Doc Finnerty says she is."

"Doc Finnerty should limit himself to one pint of the dark stuff." Kellan turned to Riley and Nan sitting at the end of the bar. Jordan was with them, the remains of their dinner littering the surface in front of them. "She is not a mermaid. She's just some girl who got drunk and ended up on the beach."

"Doc Finnerty says she doesn't look like a normal girl," Riley said.

"She was half frozen to death. Almost blue from the cold," Kellan explained. "Now I need some dinner." He glanced over at Danny. "Pack up some stew and some shepherd's pie. And soup. Lots of soup."

"You sure she wouldn't want a bucket of herring?" Danny teased.

"Just get my dinner," Kellan said.

Though he usually enjoyed his brothers' good-natured ribbing, he didn't want to turn this whole episode into something more than it was. He'd done a good deed and rescued a damsel in distress. And tomorrow, she'd find her way home and his life would get back to normal.

Danny poured him a Guinness before he went back into the kitchen to place Kellan's dinner order. A few moments later, Jordan and Nan sidled up to him, sitting down on stools on either side of him.

"Don't even ask," he growled.

"You told me you'd do the programs for our wedding ceremony," Nan said.

"Get Danny to do it," Kellan said. "He's a far better artist than I am."

"He hates using a computer. And he and Jordan are helping with the decorations." She reached over the bar to retrieve a box. "Please?"

Kellan smiled. "Of course I'll do them."

Nan clapped, her expression brightening. "There's plenty of paper. You'll have to print it all on one page and then fold the page in half and then punch it at the top and string the ribbon through. And then glue a tiny little red jewel on the end of each ribbon. But be careful not to get a lot of glue on it. And let it dry before you fold it again." She paused, forcing a smile. "It's easy. Really."

"Where's she from?" Jordan asked, unable to contain her curiosity.

Kellan shrugged. "No clue."

"She must be from close by," Jordan commented. "She knew how to get down to the cove. Danny says you three are the only ones who know where the path is."

Kellan took a sip of his beer, then slowly set it down in front of him. He did know of one other person who'd discovered the path. It had been so long ago, fifteen years, more or less. The girl he'd chased across the meadow. His first kiss. He'd seen her that day and then never again. And though his memory was a bit muddled, there was something about Gelsey that was oddly familiar.

"She could use some clothes," Kellan said. "I was hoping one of you might have something to lend her."

"Is she naked up there?" Jordan asked, her eyes wide.

"No, I gave her some of my clothes. But they'll be far too large for her."

"I can run home right now," Nan offered.

"I'm sure I can find something for her," Jordan said.

"Tomorrow morning will be fine," Kellan said. "I don't think she's going anywhere tonight."

Nan leaned closer, lowering her voice. "Was she wearing a red cap? Or a cloak? You can tell us. We won't say anything."

"I wouldn't have expected you to fall for all that mermaid rubbish," Kellan said. "She was wearing a green silk dress with nothing underneath."

"Hmm," Nan said, her brow furrowed. "The Irish legends about merrows say that they wear a red cap or a cloak and if the human steals either one, the merrow will forget her life in the sea and live on land with the human."

"If you want to keep her, maybe you should start looking for that cloak or hat," Jordan teased. "I'd definitely hide the green silk dress for safe measure."

"Yeah, I'll get right on that," Kellan said with a chuckle. "Because the best way to form a perfect relationship is to trap someone into staying with me. Especially some magical sea creature that isn't human in the first place."

Nan and Jordan giggled. "So she's probably not a real merrow," Nan said. "But if she's pretty and you like her, maybe you should ask her to stay a little longer. You need a date to our engagement party, don't you?"

He smiled. "I really don't think she'll hang around that long."

By the time he finished his beer, Danny had packed up his supper order in a paper sack and encouraged him to bring the "merrow" down to the pub for lunch the following day. Kellan put up with the last bit of teasing before making his escape.

As he walked back to the cottage, the wind nipped at his face. The thought that Gelsey might have died on the beach sent a shiver running through him. How long had she been there? Was there no one who'd missed her? Wouldn't her absence cause at least one person to wonder where she was sleeping for the night?

The cottage was dark and quiet when he stepped inside. The peat fire on the hearth had cooled and Kellan set the bag of food and box of paper on the table and slipped out of his jacket. When he saw Gelsey on the sofa, sound asleep, he kicked off his shoes and crossed to the hearth.

He silently tossed another brick of peat on the fire, then turned and looked at her. The light from the flame played across her beautiful face and he studied her for a long moment. Was she the girl he remembered from so long ago? If it was her, where had she been all this time? Why hadn't he seen her in the last fifteen years?

A sudden thought occurred to him and he walked into the bedroom and bent down at a spot beneath the window. The floorboard was still loose. He took his keys out of his pocket and pried the end up, peering into the dark space between the joists.

There it was. Where he'd hidden it all those years ago. Kellan reached down and pulled out the old biscuit tin, wiping the dust away with his palm. Did it belong to her? Is that why she'd come back to him? Or was he just fooling himself that there was something special about her?

Kellan sat down on the bed and pried off the lid, silently inventorying the contents and looking for a clue about the previous owner. When he found nothing, he tucked the tin into the bottom drawer of the bedside table, then walked to the kitchen and grabbed a cold beer.

Stretching out in the overstuffed chair across from the sofa, he watched her, thinking about what it would be like to have her in his bed. The heat from the hearth relaxed him and he sensed that whatever happened between them would be incredibly pleasurable.

This wasn't a woman who hid her passions. Whatever had sent her to that beach last night, dressed in almost nothing, and vulnerable to the wind and cold, had overwhelmed all common sense. Who or what had driven her to nearly kill herself?

He silently catalogued what he knew about her. She

was familiar enough with the area to know how to get down to the cove. He'd already ruled out the possibility that she'd washed ashore from the water. She wasn't wearing any underwear with her dress, so she probably hadn't been out in public before visiting the beach. She wasn't a local. Her accent was an odd mix of British and American and something else. Something more exotic.

She seemed well educated, maybe even coming from a posh background, though he wasn't sure what brought him to that conclusion. Maybe it was in the way she moved, with such self-assured grace and perfect posture. And in the way she ate, quietly sipping her soup from the spoon as if dining in some fancy restaurant.

Kellan sat in front of the fire for a long time, thinking about the women who'd populated his past. He'd always carefully chosen those he invited into his bed. Vulnerability wasn't a quality he sought. But looking at Gelsey, he felt a strange urge to protect her, to keep her from harm.

When he finished his beer, he got up and took the empty to the kitchen, then wandered back to the bedroom. He thought about waking her, but she seemed quite comfortable on the sofa.

He stripped off his clothes in the dark, then flopped down on the bed, dressed only in his boxers. He closed his eyes, but images of Gelsey plagued his thoughts. His fingers twitched as he remembered the feel of her naked body beneath his palms, recalled the soft swell of her breasts, the sweet curve of her backside. Just the thought of touching her brought an unwelcome reaction and Kellan groaned and rolled over on his stomach.

Unless he wanted to put up with this kind of torment for the rest of his stay in Ballykirk, he'd have to return Gelsey to where she belonged. He pulled the pillow over his head and quietly sang a familiar pub song that went on and on.

Like counting sheep, the song gradually relaxed him and he found himself drifting closer and closer to sleep. The image in his head slowly morphed into a dream as sleep overcame him.

THE WIND RATTLED the windows and Gelsey sat up and ran her hands through her tangled hair. Where was she? She squinted to see in the low light from the hearth. This wasn't her room at Winterhill. Or her room at her mother's apartment on Park Avenue. She didn't recognize anything.

She swung her feet off the sofa and stood, fighting a wave of dizziness. Running her hands over her clothes, she remembered that she was in Kellan Quinn's house. What time was it? How long had she slept? And where was Kellan?

The room was chilly and she rubbed her arms, then grabbed up the quilt and wrapped it around her body. She was normally a restless sleeper, preferring to nap during the day and stay awake during the darkest hours. Rain hissed at the windows and she crossed the room to the fireplace.

There was no more peat to feed the fire and the room

would only get colder. She raked her hands through her hair again, then wandered over to the bedroom, her bare feet silent on the rough wooden floor.

She found Kellan asleep in the bed, his form faintly visible in the dark. His long legs were twisted around the bedclothes and his arm was thrown over his head, his naked chest bare to the chilly room. Gelsey stood over him, deciding whether she ought to wake him, or just crawl into bed beside him.

She tossed the quilt over the bed, then stretched out along the length of his body. As she slipped under the covers, he jerked, then pushed up on his elbow, squinting into the dark.

"The fire went out," she whispered. "It's cold out there."

He cleared his throat. "I—I can fetch more peat," he said. "And there's a portable heater in the kitchen."

"This is all right," she said. "You're warm." She snuggled into that warmth. He had a beautiful body, slender but muscular, perfectly masculine in every way.

He grabbed her hand, pressing it to his heart and Gelsey felt his pulse beneath her palm, quick and sure. She held her breath, wondering what was going through his mind. "Maybe I should go find that heater," she murmured.

"No." Kellan held tight to her hand. "It's all right. You can stay."

She relaxed again and stretched out beside him. "I love nights like this," Gelsey whispered, "listening to the rain and the wind outside. It makes me feel safe, all warm and cozy and out of the weather."

"You weren't out of the weather last night," he said.

"I wasn't out there all night," Gelsey explained. "I walked out there after the sun came up."

"You were drunk at seven in the morning?"

"Not so much drunk as just…drained. Emotionally exhausted."

"Would you like to tell me why?"

Gelsey shook her head. That was the last thing she wanted to talk about. There was nothing about her past that she wanted to remember. "It's not important." She pushed up on an elbow and tried to make out his features in the dark. "Thank you for coming to my rescue. I don't know if I said that before, but I do appreciate what you did."

"Not a problem," Kellan said.

She leaned closer to kiss him on the cheek, but at the last moment, he turned and her lips came down on the corner of his mouth. Gelsey froze. She'd promised herself that she wasn't going to rush headlong into a sexual relationship again. She was going to think before she acted.

But Kellan made the next move and she was powerless to stop. He slipped his palms around her waist and pulled her beneath him. A sigh escaped from her throat as his mouth covered hers in a long and mind-numbing kiss.

Gelsey moaned softly as he stretched her arms out above her head. He was nearly naked and she was bundled up in a fleece sweatshirt and a pair of his cotton boxers. But she was glad for the barrier between them, at least for the moment. It was just a kiss and nothing more. Just a kiss, she reminded herself.

"Are you sure about this?" he whispered.

Then again, maybe it was something more. She arched against him, her movement instinctive. "I don't know," she said, the answer coming with a gasp.

Her hands skimmed over his back, her fingers exploring the rippled muscle that shifted with every movement of his body. Though she was ready to tear her clothes off, Kellan seemed more intent on seducing her slowly.

"Tell me to stop," he murmured.

But as his hands slipped beneath her clothes, Gelsey knew the battle was already lost. Desperate to feel that connection with another human being, she couldn't bring herself to say it. It was always this way with her, craving that intimacy she only found in bed with men. It wasn't always the right thing to do, but it was the only time she felt wanted and needed—and completely in control.

"Don't stop," she said, reaching for the hem of her sweatshirt.

"Relax." He took her hand and wove his fingers through hers, drawing it up to his lips. "We have time. Unless you're going to wander out into this storm all by yourself again."

Gelsey wriggled out from beneath him, then got up on her knees. "Maybe I should take my clothes off?"

"No," he said, shaking his head.

"I could take your clothes off," she suggested.

"No." He pulled her back down on top of him. "I get the feeling you usually take charge in the bedroom."

"No," Gelsey said. She paused. "Yes." He was right. She usually did do the seducing. The men she chose to seduce were always happy to be along for the ride. "But I've been told I'm really good."

"I've been told the same thing," Kellan said. He slipped his hand beneath her sweatshirt, running his palm along her belly until he cupped her breast. Gelsey's breath caught in her throat as his thumb grazed her nipple. "I do know what I'm doing. If you just trust me, I'm sure we'll make it through just fine."

She closed her eyes and tipped her head back as delicious sensation pulsed through her body. "Yes, I suppose we will."

He moved to the other breast. "And hasn't anyone ever told you that anticipation can sometimes be as much fun as the act itself?"

"No," she said. "In fact, you do more talking than anyone I've ever been with."

This brought a chuckle. He slipped his hands around her and pulled her back down on top of him. "Everyone in town thinks you're a mermaid."

Gelsey laughed softly. "Do you think I am?"

He slipped his hand around her nape and pulled her close. "Sweetheart, right now, I'll believe anything you tell me."

Kellan grabbed the hem of her sweatshirt and in one

smooth motion pulled it over her head and tossed it aside. He drew her closer, his lips teasing at her nipple. Gelsey sighed, furrowing her hands through his thick hair and arching against him. Inhaling deeply, she closed her eyes and relaxed, focusing on his touch.

As promised, Kellan took his time, slowly seducing her, learning what she liked, what made her shudder and what made her moan. No man had ever taken so much care to make her feel wanted. Sex had always been a race to the end. But this was a long, lazy stroll.

By the time they were both naked, Gelsey wasn't even in charge of her own reactions. As he kissed his way from her lips to her belly, she trembled, knowing exactly what was coming.

But he teased her a little longer, moving lower to gently kiss the inside of her thighs. When he finally found the spot between her legs, Gelsey was so close to the edge she knew she would lose control at the first caress. But, as if he read her distress, Kellan began slowly and deliberately.

Again and again, he brought her close, then slowly pulled back. He knew the signs of her impending release and never allowed her to tumble over the edge. A delicious tension grew inside her and with each flick of his tongue, she began to feel herself losing touch with reality.

Her fingers and toes tingled and her arms and legs felt boneless. She begged him to stop teasing and to give her what she needed, but Kellan seemed determined to prove his point. Her body belonged to him, at least for this one night and he was going to bend it to his will.

Gelsey finally ceded all control—she realized that fighting him was no use. All he wanted was to give her pleasure—deep, shattering, soul-stirring pleasure. And for the first time in her life, she trusted a man enough to allow it.

Though she didn't really know him, she sensed that he had no ulterior motive. He had no idea who she was or where she came from. He didn't know about her family or her money. And all the emotional baggage that she carried around was invisible to him, at least for now.

With this man, this stranger, she felt liberated. There were no fears hiding just beneath the surface, no doubts or insecurities. And when her release came, it was a perfect expression of what she felt—complete freedom.

Her body tensed and then dissolved into powerful spasms. He'd been right all along. It was worth the wait. Wave after wave of pleasure washed over her until she couldn't respond anymore. But though the orgasm relaxed her, it also invigorated her. And when the last shudder was long gone, Gelsey was far from finished.

Kellan pulled her into the curve of his naked body, resting his chin on her shoulder, his breath warm against her ear. Gelsey wriggled her backside, testing the limits of his control. He was hard. She could feel it. But Kellan had other ideas.

"Go to sleep," he murmured.

"I've been sleeping all day," Gelsey replied.

"I haven't. And we have a busy day ahead of us to-morrow."

"What are we doing?"

"I have no idea. But I'm sure we'll have fun. I suspect it will require a lot of energy, though."

Gelsey smiled to herself and snuggled a little closer. She didn't need to hear anything else. She had another day and maybe another night to spend in this world, with this man. And that was all she really wanted.

"You can't resist me forever," she said.

"I can't?"

"No," she whispered. There'd come a moment when he'd ache for the touch of her hand or the feel of her mouth on his body. And then, she'd give him what he'd given her…sweet, shattering release. And after that—they'd see what happened. Right now, the possibilities seemed endless.

KELLAN ROLLED OVER in bed, stretching his arms over his head. His legs were tangled in the bed linens and he kicked them aside, then reached out to Gelsey. But the opposite side of the bed was cold and empty. He sat up and drew a deep breath. The soft sound of her voice drifted in through the open door. It sounded as if she was talking on the phone.

Kellan glanced over at the clock on the bedside table. It was just past 5:00 a.m. and dawn was still hours away. Swinging his legs over the edge of the bed, Kellan stood and tiptoed to the door. A floorboard creaked beneath his feet and he paused, waiting to see if she'd noticed.

"Really," Gelsey whispered. "I'm fine. I'm safe. I'm with friends. I just didn't want you to worry."

After a long silence, she spoke again. "Yes, I have everything I need for now."

Who was she speaking to? It sounded like a parent. But maybe it was a boyfriend. Or a husband.

"I—I lost my mobile," Gelsey said. "If Antonio calls again, tell him...tell him that..." She cursed softly. "Just put him off. Don't tell him anything." She paused again. "All right. I know you do. Take care."

He heard her set the phone back into the cradle. By the time she returned to the bed, his eyes were closed and the sheets pulled up around his waist. She sank down beside him and a moment later, he felt the warmth from her naked body against his. Kellan wrapped his arms around her and nuzzled his face into the curve of her neck.

"Are you awake?" she whispered.

"I wasn't...until now. Where were you?"

"Bathroom," she lied. Gelsey shuddered and wriggled back against him, her backside nestled into his lap. "I'm so cold. I just can't seem to stay warm."

It was a blatant invitation to touch her, to run his hands over her bare skin. Kellan considered his options. Why even bother to resist, he mused. She was offering herself to him without any conditions. Why not enjoy her company while she was here? He reached out and smoothed his hand over her shoulder, pushing her hair aside until he could kiss the curve of her neck.

The warmth of his lips on her skin was enough to get him aroused again, enough to make him forget all his doubts about who she was and where she came from. In truth, the mystery about this woman made it even more exciting, more dangerous.

She turned to face him and almost immediately, her mouth found his. She kissed him without any hesitation, her tongue tangling with his as he pulled her beneath his naked body. Everything about her was perfect, her long, slender limbs, her pale silken skin, the addictive taste of her lips….

Kellan groaned as she slid her leg up along his hip, his growing erection cradled at the juncture of her thighs. It would be so simple to just slip inside her and he ached to join in this way, to share such an intimate connection.

He hadn't planned on unplanned sex. Part of the reason he'd focused on her earlier was that he wasn't really sure he had any condoms with him. He usually kept a box in the side pocket of his duffel, but he'd put his emptied bag in the boot of his car to get it out of the way.

Gelsey pressed her palm to his chest. Kellan was sure she could feel his heart slamming against it. He'd always had such control around women, trying to figure out what they wanted, and what he was willing to surrender to get what he wanted. It was like a chess game, only with naked bodies and unsatisfied desires.

But he didn't want to think now. He just wanted to feel. And when Gelsey ran her palm between them, then wrapped her fingers around his shaft, Kellan closed his eyes and groaned. He didn't know anything about her, except her name. And one other thing. She could make his body ache like no other women ever had.

"I need to go get a condom," he murmured.

"You don't keep them in the bedroom?"

"They're in my duffel. I think."

"Where is your duffel?"

"In my car." Cursing softly, Kellan crawled out of bed. This would no doubt prove to her that he wasn't the smoothest guy on the planet.

"Aren't you going to put some clothes on?" she asked.

He shook his head. "No. That will take too long. I'm just going to make a run for it." Kellan hurried to the front door, grabbing his keys from the table as he passed. With a squeal of excitement, Gelsey followed him, tugging the quilt off the bed and wrapping it around them both.

"You don't have to come with me," he said. "It's freezing out there."

He wrapped his arm around her waist and pulled her body against his, kissing her deeply as his hand skimmed over her bare torso. When they finally pulled the front door open, a cold, wet wind hit them both in the face. Gelsey covered him with the blanket and stood in the doorway, naked and shivering. "Run," she cried. "Hurry."

Drawing a deep breath, Kellan started down the garden path. The bricks were freezing and slick under his feet and by the time he reached his car, he was already soaked. Fumbling with the keys, he tried to keep the quilt wrapped around himself, but a gust caught it and exposed his nude body to the full brunt of the storm.

When he reached the front door, duffel in his hand, Gelsey was waiting with a towel. She rubbed the rain from his face and hair, then slammed the door shut and gently pulled him along to the fireplace.

"It's bloody cold out there."

"You're stark naked," she said with a giggle. "What did you expect?"

He glanced down. "I think I've done irreparable damage to my manhood."

Gelsey looked up at him, sending him a coy smile. "I can take care of that."

As she continued to dry him off, he reached out and cupped her cheek in his palm. "Who are you? What are you doing here with me?"

"I'm not sure," she said. "But I do know that I don't want to leave yet."

He brought her lips to his and kissed her, a rush of warmth snaking through his body. It wasn't enough to possess only her mouth. Kellan pulled her against him, stumbling back against the door and dropping the leather duffel.

Grabbing her hips, he spun them around and pressed her against the door. Gelsey slipped her hand between them and slowly began to stroke. She'd been right all along. She had a very simple antidote for the cold. In little more than a minute, he was hard and ready and aching to bury himself in her warmth.

Outside, the weather raged, the wind roaring up from the sea and the rain pelting at the windowpanes. But inside the cottage, they found the storm between them just as powerful and overwhelming.

Kellan's mouth savaged Gelsey's and he felt himself losing all sense of control. The last time had been gentle and slow, but this time he didn't want to wait. For Kellan, there was no longer any point in pretending. Since he'd held her body against his on the beach, he'd known this moment would come. It felt as if he'd been waiting for this his entire adult life—waiting for a woman who could make him feel real raw passion.

"Condom," he murmured.

She reached down and picked up his duffel and he rummaged through it until he found the box. Saying a silent prayer that it wasn't empty, Kellan opened it. A single foil packet fell into his palm. "Stroke of luck there," he murmured.

Gelsey grabbed the packet and tore it open, then quickly sheathed him. She drew him along to the sofa, then pushed him down, straddling his hips with her knees. Gently, she guided him inside her. He wanted to slow down, to just take a moment and enjoy the anticipation. But the instant he felt her warmth close around him, Kellan was lost. He held his breath, marshaling his control, trying to fix his mind on something other than the woman above him.

Programs, he thought to himself. He had to do those damn wedding programs. Ribbon and little red jewels, Nan had said. He didn't know what the hell she'd been talking about, but as long as he focused on his brother's wedding plans, he'd be all right.

"Do you want me to move?" she whispered, her words soft against his ear.

"No," he said.

"It works better if I move."

He leaned back and found her smiling down at him. "I know. I have done this before."

"Really? It's hard to tell."

Chuckling softly, he clasped her hips and moved. "Better?"

"Do it again," she said with a laugh.

He did as she asked and she groaned softly. "See how good that feels?"

She leaned over him and touched her lips to his. "You were right," she whispered.

"About what?"

"You *are* very good at this."

# 3

GELSEY SNUGGLED into the soft covers of the bed. It was still warm with the heat from Kellan's body, even though he'd gotten up an hour before. She was beginning to feel almost normal and attributed part of that to the passionate interlude she'd shared with her rescuer.

Sex had always been an important part of Gelsey's life, but never for the right reasons. According to a long string of therapists, she used sex to create a false sense of security, the security she'd never enjoyed as a child.

Her early childhood had been spent with her nanny, Marie, a wonderful Frenchwoman who had been more of a mother than Dorothy Trent Woodson had ever been. And Gelsey had been happy with that life, even if she rarely spent time with her parents.

But after the divorce, Marie had been sent away, there one day and gone the next. And Gelsey had been packed and shipped off to a Swiss boarding school, a place where she was to be well educated and carefully prepared to take her place in society as some billionaire's charming wife.

At first, she'd accepted her fate and done her best at school. But then, she'd discovered boys. And along with boys came a sense of exhilarating freedom. There was nothing to stop her from living her life exactly how she chose. That first spontaneous kiss with Kellan had been just the start of her pursuit of pleasure.

Thinking back on it, it had been a terribly bold move on her part. But her grandmother had always told her that if she wanted to be happy, she had to grab happiness wherever she could find it. At that moment in time, Kellan had represented everything that was wonderful about life.

She'd watched him and his brothers from afar, hidden behind the rocks on the cliff. He'd been the one she'd fashioned her silly schoolgirl dreams around, the dark, brooding, handsome boy with the pale blue eyes and the confident air about him.

He'd been her first, but he hadn't been her last. Schoolgirl fantasies gave way to teenage realities. Once back in Switzerland, she'd begun to sneak out after curfew. A few years later, there were ski weekends with college boys, older brothers of her schoolmates. She quickly learned to use her sex appeal to get whatever she wanted from handsome men.

After being kicked out of one boarding school, her parents sent her to another and another. It was then she discovered that bad behavior was all it took to get attention from her parents.

Prep school was followed by university. She headed for Paris and studied art history at the Sorbonne, cooking at Le Cordon Bleu and apprenticed as a designer at Studio Berçot. Then she gained access to her trust fund and her life as a celebutante began.

Gelsey sighed and pulled the covers over her head. She was so tired of that life, completely exhausted playing the role she'd created for herself. The men, the money, the parties. It had all become a giant, crashing bore. And now she'd found an escape, a place to breathe, to take stock of the future and put her past behind her.

To the rest of the world, she was Gigi Woodson. She dated famous athletes and gorgeous male models and sexy actors. She moved from one man to another whenever she grew bored or restless. And every now and then, she got so drunk that she did something that landed her in the tabloids. But here, on the western coast of Ireland, she was a stranger without a past.

Very few people knew her well. Her parents had never bothered to try. But her grandmother had always been able to see inside her heart and say the words that made her feel loved and cherished. It had been the only truly good thing she'd remembered from her childhood. Gelsey felt emotion tighten her throat and she fought back the tears. If only her grandmother were here now, to help her through, to reassure her.

A knock sounded at the front door and Gelsey pushed up, bracing her hand beneath her. She raked her tousled hair out of her eyes and searched around for something to wear. The sweatshirt that Kellan had given her the night before was draped over the bedpost. She grabbed it and pulled it over her head, then tugged on his boxer shorts.

The house was warmer, a fresh peat fire burning in the hearth and the little space heater humming away in the corner. She pulled the door open expecting to see Kellan, his arms overloaded with breakfast. But two women were standing outside, friendly smiles pasted on their faces.

"Hello," Gelsey said, rubbing the sleep from her eyes. "I'm afraid Kellan isn't here."

"Better that," the brunette said cheerfully. "We've come to see you." She held a canvas bag in front of her. "We've brought you something to wear. I'm Jordan and this is Nan."

The raven-haired woman held out another bag. "And you must be Gelsey."

Gelsey stepped away from the door and the two strolled inside as if they were quite at home. Nan wrinkled her nose, then motioned toward the fire. "We really should talk to the boys about putting in central heat. Those peat fires make my eyes water."

"And they should put in a decent bathroom. That shower isn't any bigger than a broom closet."

"Could I offer either of you a cup of tea?" Gelsey asked. Although she'd been well schooled in etiquette, she wasn't quite sure what to do with strangers bearing gifts of secondhand clothing.

Nan stared at her for a long moment. "Have we met?"

"I'm sure we haven't," Gelsey said.

"You look so familiar." Nan plopped down on the end of the sofa. "Now, I'm not sure you'll like anything I brought. But Kellan said you didn't have any decent clothes to wear. I brought a pair of jeans and a couple sweaters—or jumpers, as he calls them. It's so damp in the winter."

"And I brought a jacket," Jordan said. "It's not very fashionable, but it will be warm. And underwear. It's new, still in the package."

Nan rummaged through her bag. "And I have gloves and a hat. And boots. Did you bring the boots, Jo?"

They were both talking so fast that Gelsey could do nothing more than nod and smile. When they finally finished, she drew a ragged breath. "And you're from… the church?"

"Oh, Kellan didn't tell you we'd be stopping by? He saw us both last night at the pub and explained your situation. I'm engaged to Kellan's brother Riley."

"They're getting married New Year's Eve. And I'm with Danny, the other brother."

"Right," Gelsey said. "I remember now." She frowned. "You're not Irish."

"American," Nan said. "And you're not Irish, either."

"No," Gelsey said. She thought it best to leave it at that, unwilling to go into a long explanation of her life. "Let me just put the water on for tea."

"Oh, we can't stay," Nan said. "We're on our way to Cork. I'm shopping for a wedding dress."

"Shopping," Gelsey murmured. She'd been an expert at that in her former life.

"You wouldn't want to come with, would you?" Nan asked.

Jordan clapped her hands. "You should come! We'll make a girls' day of it. And it will get you out of this cottage." She paused and the color rose on her cheeks. "That is, if you want to leave. But I can completely understand why you wouldn't. I'm sure Kell is keeping you—"

"Busy," Nan finished.

"I can't. I'm a bit broke right now."

The two women stared at her with uneasy smiles. "Perfectly understandable," Nan said. "Why would you have any use for— I mean, you've spent your life…"

"Living in the ocean," Jordan said.

"What— Oh!" Gelsey laughed. "Right. Kellan told me that everyone thinks I'm a mermaid."

Jordan nodded. "Of course, we don't really believe that. But when in Ireland…"

"I love that about Ireland," Gelsey said. "People still believe in magic here."

"And you do look the part, with all that long, wavy hair," Nan said. "Danny was right. You are beautiful."

"Danny?"

"He was there when Kellan rescued you," Jordan explained.

A slow smile curled the corners of Gelsey's mouth

and she shrugged. "I don't really remember meeting him."

"What size are your feet?" Jordan asked.

"Eight?" Gelsey said.

"Perfect! The boots are eight and a half. Just wear extra socks. Are you sure you won't come with us? We'll have lunch. Our treat."

"Maybe another time," Gelsey said. "Really. I'd love to go another time."

They both stood. "Good," Nan said. "I'm sure we'll see you around the pub. Tell Kellan to bring you down for dinner tonight."

Gelsey took the offered bags and walked them to the door. This was all very strange. Gelsey couldn't remember the last time she'd been able to be completely anonymous. No matter where she went, someone always recognized her.

But then, she was usually dressed quite differently and hiding behind an image that was regularly splashed across the pages of the tabloids. For the first time in a very long time, she had a chance to live life like an ordinary woman.

She had a fresh start, a chance to make real friends who didn't care about her notoriety or her money or her family connections. And Nan and Jordan seemed exactly like the kind of women she'd want for friends.

After she said goodbye, Gelsey quickly found an outfit to wear, then pulled on socks and the soft fleece-lined boots. Though she was a bit taller than Nan and Jordan, with longer arms, she couldn't complain. It was good enough to go out in public in and she needed some fresh air and exercise.

She'd walk down to the village and get her bearings. If she was going to stay for a while, she needed a source of income. She could just go get her bank cards at Winterhill, but if she was going to start over, then she needed to find a way to make a living. She needed a job.

But could she survive on her own? It was a challenge she'd never have thought of taking on in the past, but now it made sense. Gigi Woodson, celebrity heiress, was gone and Gelsey Woodson, ordinary working girl, had been born. For once, she didn't want to mess it all up.

Gelsey grabbed the jacket from the sofa and slipped into it. When she opened the door, the chilly air rushed in and she drew a deep breath and smiled. It was a beautiful day. She had no idea what was going to happen, but it was exciting to be completely unsure of her future.

She followed the road down to the village at a brisk walk, smiling to herself as she took in the beauty of the countryside. Everything looked so picturesque— the vivid green hills and the whitewashed village set against the slate-blue sea. Boats bobbed in the harbor and she watched one as it slowly moved out into the bay.

Gelsey had lived in many exotic places, but she'd never felt at home. Maybe this was where she'd belonged all along. She was destined to find Kellan all these years later and to begin where they'd left off as teenagers.

KELLAN SQUINTED against the late-morning sun as he drove out of Ballykirk toward the cottage. He'd left Gelsey naked and sound asleep in his bed. After last night, he'd figured she'd need her sleep. But it was nearly noon and he'd fetched lunch from the pub, hoping that they could spend the rest of the day in bed after a hearty meal.

It was the perfect day to spend curled up beneath the sheets, he mused. A winter chill had set in and the damp wind blowing off the sea made it feel colder than it was. Christmas was three weeks away and after that, the new year. He'd made a resolution last year on New Year's Eve to expand his professional horizons, to take jobs outside of Ireland and see a bit more of the world. And here he was, just a month away from his deadline and he still hadn't made a decision about the project in France.

As he rounded a bend in the road, Kellan caught sight of a figure striding toward him. As he drove closer, he recognized Gelsey, her pale hair blowing in the wind. She smiled and waved. He pulled the car to a stop and rolled down the window.

"What are you doing out here?"

"A couple of your friends brought me some clothes." She pointed to her feet. "And boots. I was coming to find you."

"Hop in," he said, leaning across the seat to open the passenger-side door.

She joined him inside the car, her color high, her eyes bright. Kellan knew she was a beautiful woman, but the sight of her in broad daylight was enough to take his breath away. An unbidden surge of hunger raced through him and he fought his instinct to drag her into his arms and kiss her. "So, I guess you slept well last night. You're clearly feeling better."

"I feel wonderful," Gelsey said. "Good sex always does that for me."

Kellan couldn't help but smile. "And what would you like to do today? I have lunch." He pointed to the paper sack in the backseat.

"Well, we could eat." She paused as she considered her options. "And then, I'd like..."

"What?"

"I'd like you to teach me how to drive this car."

"You don't know how to drive?"

"I never had a reason to."

Kellan groaned. "Don't start with that mermaid bollocks again. I know you're not a mermaid."

"I was going to say that I never had a reason to learn," she said. A tiny smile quirked at the corners of her mouth. "We don't have cars at the bottom of the ocean. And it's really difficult to work the pedals with flippers."

Kellan laughed. "I'll teach you how to drive if you tell me the truth about where you come from."

"Why? There's nothing wrong with exercising your imagination every now and then. Is it so hard to believe I came from the sea?"

"Why can't you tell me the truth? Is that so hard to do?"

She stared out the windscreen, her gaze fixed on the landscape passing by. "Have you ever wanted to change your life? Just start all over again?"

"I wish I could go back and change a few things," Kellan said.

She looked at him, curiosity filling her eyes. "Like what?"

"I had a chance to go into business with a developer a few years ago, to buy properties and fix them up and then sell them. I thought it was too risky, but now I'm thinking that risk might not be such a bad thing."

"Why don't you do it now?" she asked.

"I get paid a boatload to do exactly what I do best," he said, shaking his head. "And the economy hasn't been too good. In the end, I was right to trust my instincts."

"I always liked to take risks," she said. "It makes life more exciting."

"Or more chaotic," Kellan countered.

"A little chaos might be good for you," she said.

"You don't know me very well."

Gelsey smiled. "I'm a really good judge of people. It's one of my most amazing qualities."

"But you can't drive," he said.

"I'm not perfect," she teased.

"Close," Kellan replied. "All right, switch spots with me and we'll give this a go. You have to promise to listen to everything I say."

She crawled over him, stopping at the point where

she straddled his legs. "This is nice," she murmured, her breasts in his face.

"It's impossible to drive this way," he murmured, staring up at her, his gaze fixed on her lips. With a groan, Kellan shoved his fingers through the hair at her nape and dragged her into a long, deep kiss. This hunger for the taste of her was so difficult to deny, especially when she was so available and so willing.

When she finally drew back, a satisfied smile curled her lips. "Is that a gearshift in your pocket or are you just happy to see me?" she teased. Gelsey giggled as she moved over him, taunting him with the friction of her body against his. "I see I've got your engine running, don't I?"

Kellan held up his hands, chuckling softly. "Stop. The metaphors are torture enough. Do you want to learn to drive?"

"Yes," she said. "As long as we can get back to this lesson later."

"And what lesson is that?"

"The lesson that teaches you that you can't possibly resist me."

Kellan groaned. "I believe I learned that lesson the first day we met."

"And it's my duty to keep reminding you," she said.

There was no need to do that, Kellan mused. It was painfully evident the effect she had on his body. A single kiss was enough to set him off. But his reaction hadn't been just physical. He was developing a real affection for Gelsey.

She was smart and witty and managed to drag him out of his serious nature with just a smile. When he was with her, he didn't dwell on his professional worries. Hell, he'd barely thought about work at all. He liked the fact that he actually had a personal life now, a reason to relax and take time off.

But how long could that possibly last? Kellan wondered. Would there come a point where they grew bored with each other, where being together seemed more like a chore than a treat?

"Switch!" Gelsey said. When she'd finally settled herself behind the wheel, she glanced over at him. "Where are we going to go?"

"Back to the cottage."

Gelsey shook her head. "No, I want to go into town."

"But I have lunch right here. It's going to get cold."

"I'm not hungry. I need to look for a job."

Kellan frowned, taken aback by her request. "A job? What exactly is a mermaid qualified to do?"

"I don't know. I'm very good with people, I'm clever and I'm a fast learner. I expect I could do any number of jobs. Do you need a waitress at the pub? I could do that. And I can also cook. I'm a very good cook."

"You cook?"

She stared out the windscreen and nodded, her attention now absorbed with learning to drive. "I am very good with fish. It's my specialty." She looked at him and grinned. "Really. I'll cook you dinner sometime." Gelsey grabbed the gearshift and put it into Drive. "Ready?"

"Buckle your safety belt," he warned.

She did as she was told, then clutching the wheel, she slowly pressed on the accelerator. To Kellan's surprise, the car glided smoothly forward. After only a few minutes, he had reason to suspect that she'd driven before. Though she appeared a bit tense, she knew exactly what she was doing.

They came to a crossroad north of Ballykirk and she stopped and looked at him. "Which way?"

"You're in charge," he said. "You choose. Who taught you how to drive? Because I don't believe you've never driven before."

"A very nice octopus taught me when I was just a tadpole." She turned left, heading along the coast and for a moment, she drove on the wrong side of the road. But then, before he could speak, she corrected herself. "Sorry," she murmured. "We usually drive on the other side in…the ocean."

"You're doing well," he said.

"I'm going to need a car," she said. "How much does a car cost? I've never bought one."

"Varies," he said. "But before you get a car, you need a license. You'll have to take a test. In truth, you should have a permit now. The garda probably could stop you and—"

She slammed on the brakes and the car skidded to a stop. "That's enough for now," she said, putting the gearshift back into Park. Gelsey shoved the door open and hopped out. Kellan got out and they exchanged places.

"I didn't mean you had to stop," he said. "The garda usually doesn't patrol these roads during the day."

"I don't want to cause any trouble," she said. "I'm already in…" She paused, then pointed out the window. "Drive on."

They continued their drive along the coast and when they passed by Castle Cnoc, Kellan slowed the car and stopped at the gate. He pointed up the driveway. "That's one of my projects," he said. "Just finished last month. Jordan was the project manager."

"It's lovely," she said. "Do you like your job, then?"

"Sure. I've always loved historical properties. It's like mixing history with architecture. New buildings just don't have the same appeal to me."

"I wish I knew what I was meant to do," she murmured. "I've never had to choose a path for my life. It was chosen for me. How do you pick?"

"I didn't," he said. "It just always seemed like the right thing. You'll figure it out."

"I'm twenty-seven years old," she said.

"Is that in fish years or human years?" he teased.

"Human," she said. "Sometimes, I feel like I'm just starting my life. Like a baby taking her first steps."

An odd expression crossed her face and Kellan could only read it as regret. He knew nothing of her past or what she was running away from. But he knew that he cared enough to give her a safe place to stay for a while. "You won't need to buy a car," he said. "My family has a little Fiat that we lend out to tourists who rent the cottage. It's parked behind Danny's smithy. You can use it for as long as you like."

She glanced over at him, her expression shifting suddenly. "Thank you," she said. "That's very nice of you. But I still think I should get a car of my own."

The smile she sent him was like a ray of sunshine, warm and bright and full of everything that he needed to survive. But Kellan got the uneasy feeling that his affection for Gelsey would come at a price. The more he got to know her, the more he needed her. So what would happen when she decided to leave?

It wasn't a question that he'd thought about in any great depth, but now, the idea of losing her outweighed any fears he had of getting too close. "I suppose we could drive into town and see if anyone is looking for help."

"You really think someone would hire me?"

As Kellan turned the car around and headed back to Ballykirk, he realized that Gelsey's job hunt might provide a bit more insight into who she really was. She'd have to give a last name and if she wasn't an Irish citizen, she'd have to give a whole lot more than that.

GELSEY HAD BEEN CURIOUS about the inhabitants of Kellan's hometown, but she'd never expected them to be so curious about her. "Why is everyone staring at me?" she murmured as she and Kellan strolled down the main street of Ballykirk.

"Are they?" he asked.

"Yes! Haven't you noticed? They don't really think I'm a—"

"No," Kellan said. "I suspect they're just curious about what's going on between us. Everyone in this village is in everyone else's business. You can't sneeze in this town without a half-dozen people offering medical advice. It's kind of the same with romance."

She opened her mouth, then snapped it shut. Of course. She and Kellan been shacked up together for two days now, eating take-out food from the pub and no doubt creating all sorts of speculation. Now that they'd emerged from their den of passion, people were bound to be curious.

"I suppose I'll have to get used to that kind of thing," she murmured.

"They're just excited to have something new to gossip about. They'll move along to a new subject soon enough."

Gelsey forced a smile. Or maybe not. How long would it be before someone recognized her? Without the makeup and the skimpy dresses, she barely looked like the girl in the tabloids. But was Ballykirk really that isolated from the rest of the world? "I love this village," she said. "It's so…picturesque."

"Ballykirk? When I was a lad I couldn't wait to leave."

"You did leave," she said.

Kellan nodded. "For university. In Dublin and then a year in London."

"Why did you come back?" Gelsey asked.

"I'm not technically back. I just finished the job at Castle Cnoc and I don't have anything else lined up until after the new year. I usually live in Dublin."

"I ought to have finished university," Gelsey said. In truth, she hadn't given it much chance. She'd been too restless to sit in a class all day, so she'd decided to go to cooking school. When she'd grown bored with that, she'd tried fashion school. Paired with her lack of real work experience, she'd been left with a rather unconventional résumé.

"They have universities where you come from?" he asked. "Oh, wait. I don't know where you come from, do I?"

She slipped her arm through his and gave him a playful slap. "How do you think I learned to speak French?" she asked.

"You speak French?"

*"Mais oui,"* Gelsey replied.

"You're hiding all sorts of secrets, aren't you?"

Her expression suddenly turned serious. "We all have secrets. I suspect you have a few of your own."

"No," he said.

"None?"

"Well, when I was fourteen, I wanted to be James Bond. I mean, the bloke was a god with the women."

"And you weren't?"

"No. Far from it. I'd never kissed a girl before. And then, that summer it happened and after that it was a brand-new world."

"Tell me about it," Gelsey said.

He glanced over at her. "I suspect you know how it goes."

She drew in a sharp breath. Was he referring to the kiss they'd shared all those years before? Did he remember her? She'd been so young. Eleven years old and all arms and legs. And so flat-chested she was sure she'd never grow breasts.

"Sure," Gelsey said. "It's always very clumsy at first. But you obviously got the hang of it. In fact, you're quite an expert now."

She glanced into a shop window as they passed by and then stopped short. "Look," she said, pointing to the hand-lettered sign: Help Wanted. Enquire Within. Gelsey stepped back to look at the sign hung above the door. "Maeve Dunphrey's Potions and Lotions," she read.

"You don't want to go in there," Kellan said.

"It looks nice. And she's looking for help."

"Trust me, there are lots of other places that would be better suited."

"But this looks like fun. She sells soap and hand lotion and perfumes. I know about those things."

"All right. But before you go in, you should know that she's crazy. A complete nutter. Gone in the head. She thinks she's a Druid priestess. She makes all sorts of potions. She almost poisoned Billy Murphy with a love potion once."

"Really?" Gelsey reached for the door. "She sounds very interesting."

"And I doubt that she has any money to pay you. She

barely scrapes by and no one really visits her shop any-more. Those who do, buy her things just to be chari-table."

"Then she really needs my help," Gelsey said. She pulled the door open and stepped inside. It was apparent from the outset why her shop wasn't doing well. It was a top-to-bottom mess. Beautiful old display cases were overflowing with jars and tins and boxes of homemade beauty products. Some looked as though they'd been there for years and others were wrapped in brightly col-ored paper and tied with little bits of string.

"Hello." An elderly woman dressed in a long tap-estry robe appeared from the back of the shop. "Wel-come." She tipped her head and smiled, blinking at Gelsey through horn-rimmed glasses. "You must be the one they've been talking about. The one who came to us from the sea."

"And you must be the priestess," Gelsey replied.

"That I am." Maeve motioned her forward. "Let's have a look at you. I must say, I have been a bit curi-ous since I first heard your story from Doc Finnerty. He comes in for my sea-salt scrub. His wife loves it for her feet. Keeps them soft."

Maeve made a careful study of Gelsey, then nodded. "You're quite a beauty. I expected nothing less. It's a fortunate thing Kellan found you when he did."

"I'd like to inquire about the job," Gelsey said. "The sign in your window says you need help. And I think I could help you."

"Oh, dear. That sign has been there forever. And you're the first person who's come in."

"What are the job requirements?"

Maeve looked around. "I suppose organization would be crucial. As you can see, I'm not much with that. I need someone who is creative. I've always thought I could do a better job with my displays, but I haven't the patience or the time."

"I could do that for you," Gelsey said.

"I can't pay much and I'm not sure how long I'm going to keep the shop. I've wanted to sell it for a while now, and move to Galway to live with my sister. But with help, I might be able to shine the place up a bit."

"I'm your girl," Gelsey stated.

Maeve reached out and took her hand. "I do believe you are."

"When would you like me to start?"

"How about next week? We're closed on Mondays, so Tuesday morning. How is ten?"

"I'll be here at nine," Gelsey said. She shook Maeve's hand, but then couldn't control herself and threw her arms around the elderly woman. "You won't regret this. I promise." Embarrassed, Gelsey stepped back. "Sorry. I'm just very excited. I didn't expect it would be this simple."

"Yes. Well, having a mermaid in the shop might liven things up a bit." She paused. "Oh, and one more thing." Maeve hurried over to one of the display cases and picked up a small jar, then handed it to Gelsey. "I can see you haven't been getting much sleep lately. Try this. It does wonders for bags under the eyes."

"Thank you," Gelsey said. "I will try it tonight. And I'll see you on Tuesday."

When she walked out of the shop, Gelsey jumped into Kellan's arms and yelled, "I got a job!" She gave him a long, lingering kiss. When she finally drew back, she looked around to find several people staring at them. "Well, that will give the townsfolk something new to talk about," she said.

"Yes, I suspect it will. And congratulations—I think. Can we go home now and have some lunch?"

"All right. But I want to do something more. I'll cook for you tonight. A wonderful gourmet meal."

"That's not necessary," he said.

"But I want to." She pushed up on her toes and gave him another kiss. "This has been an amazing day. I think we need to celebrate, don't you?" Gelsey paused. "She mentioned the mermaid thing. You don't think she'll fire me once she realizes I'm not a—"

"I think everyone knows already," Kellan said. He dropped another kiss on her lips. "But that's not going to stop them from talking about it. Twenty years from now, you'll still be known as the mermaid girl."

# 4

THE ONLY LIGHT in the cottage came from the peat fire flickering on the hearth and an oil lamp Gelsey had set on the floor. Outside, a roaring wind from the sea scoured the windows. Though they had a perfectly adequate table at which to dine, Gelsey had chosen to spread their gourmet dinner out on the floor in front of the fire, creating a much more romantic atmosphere.

As Kellan poured her another glass of wine, he studied her features, still rendered breathless by her beauty. What bit of luck had brought her into his life? He could have walked in the other direction that morning. She could have climbed up the cliff on her own and disappeared again, without the two of them getting a second chance. But something had brought them together and he couldn't help but wonder if there were magical forces behind it all.

Kellan groaned inwardly. This was exactly how it began for his brothers. He'd listened to Riley and Danny tell their tales and he'd heard them both blather on and on about the incredible power of love. And now he was doing the same thing. Turning himself inside out over a woman he barely knew.

Clenching his fist, Kellan fought the urge to reach out and touch her. Was it even possible to resist anymore or was he completely lost? Yes, the sex was incredible. And he did enjoy spending time with Gelsey, talking to her and kissing her. But that didn't mean he was falling in love.

Still, he couldn't help but admit that everything that passed between them was different, as if it had been touched with something extraordinary, some little bit of magic.

She drew a deep breath and sighed, stretching her bare legs out in front of her. Gelsey was dressed in nothing but one of his oxford shirts. "I feel like a stuffed hen. I knew I could cook, but I didn't expect it would turn out so well."

"It was pretty amazing. That sauce on the salmon was incredible."

"Capers and lemon," she said, scooping up a bit on her finger and holding it out to him. "It's one of the first sauces I learned. I told you I was good with fish."

He took her finger into his mouth and enjoyed another taste of the sauce. "And potatoes. And turnips. Even the salad was perfect."

She grinned seductively, then crawled over the remnants of the meal on her hands and knees to drop a kiss on his mouth. "Are you ready for dessert?"

He glanced down, taking in the view. His shirt gaped

at the neck and he could see her bare breasts. The long tails covered her backside. "Would that involve taking your clothes off?"

"I don't know. It would most definitely involve taking all your clothes off." She reached out for the hem of his T-shirt, then pulled it over his head. Her attention focused on his chest as she smoothed her hands over his shoulders. "I've had a good day. The best day in a very long time."

Kellan nuzzled her neck. "I'm glad." He pressed his lips to a spot just below her ear. "And what made it so good?"

"Everything. And nothing at all," she said.

Kellan stared at her. "Where did you really come from, Gelsey? And why are you still here with me?"

"I think I might belong here," she said. "I don't want to go back."

"There's no one waiting for you? Wondering where you are?"

"No." She sat back on her heels and looked into his eyes. "I promise. There's no one. The only person I want to be with right now is you." She ran her hands through his hair, smoothing it away from his face. "I don't care about your past, Kellan. Nothing that happened to you before you met me makes any difference at all. We started the moment you rescued me from that beach."

"And how will we end?" he asked.

"I don't know. We don't need to worry about that right now. I'm happy and you're happy and we should leave it at that." She drew in a long breath. "You are happy, aren't you?"

Of course he was happy. What man wouldn't be? He had a beautiful, sexy woman in his bed every night, a woman who fascinated him, a woman who drove him wild with desire. And yet, he knew nothing about her. But then, maybe she was right. What difference did it make? There was very little he could learn that would change his feelings for her.

Gelsey leaned in closer. "Can I ask you a question?"

"Only if I can ask one in return," Kellan said.

"When you found me on the beach, why didn't you just take me to the hospital?"

Kellan thought about his response for a long moment. "I don't know. I guess I was curious. I wanted to know what happened, how you got on that beach and why. And I knew if I took you to the hospital, I might never see you again." He kissed her, his lips brushing against hers. "I lost you once, I didn't want to lose you again."

"You lost me?"

"My turn," Kellan said, quickly shifting the subject.

"Make it good," she warned. "You only get one."

"What really sent you out to that beach?" he asked. "It must have been something pretty upsetting."

She shook her head. "Funny, it was then, but now, I barely think about it."

"It or he? Answer the question," Kellan demanded. "Honestly. Was it a man who did that to you?"

"I did it to myself. Up until that moment, I really

didn't like the person I was. I think there's a bit of magic in you finding me on the beach. I'd like to believe there still is."

Kellan slid his fingers through her hair and drew her lips to his. She went soft in his arms and on a sigh, she parted her lips to offer him a taste. Everything about her was perfect, Kellan mused. When he touched her, sex suddenly made sense. It meant something, something deep and reassuring.

Kellan knew the risk he was taking. She'd dropped into his life so unexpectedly and he suspected she'd leave in the same way. For all he knew, he'd wake up one morning and she'd be gone. And without knowing anything about her, he'd have no way to find her again.

Grabbing her waist, he pulled her close, then threw his thigh over hers, trapping her in his embrace. He reached for the buttons of the shirt she wore and slowly undid them, kissing a path from the first bit of exposed flesh to the last.

"Who are you?" he murmured, his lips pressed against the soft flesh of her belly.

Gelsey groaned, her fingers smoothing through his hair as he moved lower. "I don't know," she whispered.

She was the woman he wanted more than any other. She was the woman whose touch could send his need over the edge. And she was the woman who was becoming a part of his life he didn't want to lose.

Kellan found the spot between her legs and gently caressed her with his tongue. Gelsey arched toward him, her fingers clenching his hair. He knew exactly how to control her release and Kellan took every advantage, knowing that it might be the only thing in their relationship that he did control. But was mind-blowing sex enough to keep her with him forever?

Her breath began to come in desperate gasps and Kellan knew she was close. He drew back and traced his way up to her neck. Her body was made for his touch, her skin so pale and smooth and her limbs long and lithe. He drew a deep breath and pulled her closer.

"Maybe we should go into the bedroom," he murmured. Kellan got to his feet and reached down to help her up. But instead of taking a step toward the bedroom, she wrapped her arms around him and kissed him, her tongue teasing at his.

"Take your clothes off," she whispered.

Kellan reached for the button of his jeans, but she was there quicker. She unzipped them, then pushed them down over his hips along with his boxers. Kellan stepped out of them, then pulled her body up against his, her shirt falling down around her elbows.

"Now that you have me naked, what are you going to do with me?"

She gazed up into his eyes, a smile twitching at the corners of her mouth. Then she grabbed his hand and dragged him toward the front door. The moment she opened the door, a huge gust blew icy-cold rain into the cottage. "It's freezing out there," he said. "And raining."

"I'm used to cold and wet," she said. Gelsey slipped out of her shirt. "Come on. Let's go commune with nature."

"Humans are not made for this kind of weather," he said, motioning down to the erection that had grown so quickly the moment he'd kissed her.

Gelsey reached down and smoothed her hand along the length of his shaft, her touch warm on his already chilly flesh. "It will heighten the experience," she murmured. Kellan reluctantly surrendered. There was obviously something in Gelsey that was fed by pushing the boundaries and taking risks. But how far would it go?

"All right."

"You first," she said.

With a shout, Kellan ran outside, his bare feet skidding on the brick walk. When he was nearly to the gate, he turned around to find Gelsey watching him from the doorway. The feeble light from the cabin outlined her nakedness so perfectly that he felt the breath slowly leave his body.

"Aren't you coming?" he shouted, the rain stinging his skin.

"No! It's freezing out there."

Kellan ran back to the door and stepped inside, pulling her along with him. "I didn't want to go out there in the first place!"

"I know," she said. "But I wanted to see how far you'd go for desire. Now I know."

"This was a test?" he asked.

She slowly slid down along his body until her hands rested on his waist. He watched as she drew her tongue along the length of his shaft, the warmth causing a rush of desire to race through him. The feel of her mouth on his cold body was like nothing he'd ever experienced before. Every nerve in his body was alive, his skin prickled with goose bumps and shivers skittering down his spine.

Kellan closed his eyes and leaned back against the door, losing himself in the feel of her mouth surrounding him, drawing him in deep and then drifting away. And when it was too much to take anymore, he pulled her to her feet and spanned her waist with his hands.

In one smooth motion, Kellan picked her up and wrapped her legs around his hips, pressing her against the door until he was positioned at the damp spot between her thighs. Slowly, he entered her, inch by inch until he was buried deep within her warmth.

"You were right," he murmured, his mouth pressed against the curve of her shoulder. "It does heighten the senses."

He drove deep and then withdrew and Gelsey gasped. "Now you can take me to bed," she whispered.

"I think I'm fine right here."

KELLAN LEFT EARLY in the morning, after he and Gelsey shared a quick breakfast together. He'd promised to help Riley with some painting at the cottage that he and Nan had just purchased in Ballykirk. Riley had hoped to have the place ready by the end of December, just in time to move in after their New Year's Eve wedding. Before leaving, he extracted a sleepy promise from Gelsey that she'd meet him for lunch at the pub.

Though Gelsey curled back up under the covers, she wasn't able to sleep. Her mind was spinning with all the possibilities that life now offered. She'd start a new job next week. She was excited at the prospect, but she was also a bit scared. She'd never held a job before. Would she actually know what to do, how to behave? What if people didn't like her? Worse yet, what if someone recognized her?

With a curse, Gelsey sat up in bed and pushed her tangled hair out of her eyes. How hard could it be to sell face creams and body lotions? But obviously Maeve didn't sell much from her shop. What if she too turned out to be a sales failure?

The first thing she needed to do was find something appropriate to wear. She couldn't go to her first day of work wearing Jordan's and Nan's hand-me-downs. She'd just have to make a quick trip back to Winterhill. Looking around the bedroom, Gelsey searched for something to write on.

She found Kellan's sketch pad on the floor next to the bed and flipped through it for a clean sheet of paper. The pencil that he'd been using last night wasn't on the floor or on the top of the nightstand. Gelsey rolled onto her stomach and pulled open the bottom drawer.

She pushed aside a rusty old tin box and searched the drawer. Then she opened the box, hoping there might be a pencil inside. Gelsey's breath caught in her throat as she recognized the objects in it. "Oh, my," she murmured, pulling out a length of braided yarn.

In a single moment, she was taken back to that day,

running through the meadow with Kellan chasing her, the old biscuit tin clutched in his hand. Time seemed to stand still as she pulled each item out of the box and examined it. These were all her magic talismans, bits and pieces of life that she'd kept for the powerful memories they held.

The day he'd chased her hadn't been the first day she'd seen him. She'd watched him from behind the rocks before, fascinated by his quiet confidence and beautiful face. He'd been her first crush, the very first boy she'd ever wanted to kiss and she'd done just that.

Gelsey smiled at the memory. She'd buried the tin just for him, hoping that he'd find it and touch something that she held dear. It was such a silly idea from a silly young girl, but now Gelsey had to wonder if the magic she believed in back then had actually worked.

She pulled out a shell and held it up to her ear, listening for the sound of the sea. If she could only go back to that time in her life, back before everything had turned upside down. Where had she gone wrong? Had there been a single event that had put her on the path she'd taken?

Her parents' divorce hadn't helped, but plenty of children survived that. Was it the endless supply of money? Had she faced her fears and insecurities rather than trying to hide them beneath a party-girl veneer, perhaps she'd have more to show for herself at age twenty-seven.

Gelsey groaned, tipping her head back and closing her eyes. All that time lost. All that money spent. And she still felt like a seabird buffeted by the wind and unable to find a place to land. What if things didn't work out in Ballykirk? What if this was just another disaster in a long line of disasters?

And how would Kellan feel about her once he found out who she really was? There'd been so many men, so many silly choices—and all of them captured in the tabloids. And the money. How could she ever justify it? It made her look so vacuous and incredibly careless.

And then there was the "incident." How would she explain that to him? She'd tried to put it out of her mind, but if things didn't go her way, she might have to spend some time in jail. Gelsey closed her eyes. How could she have been so incredibly stupid? So wrapped up in her silly little world that she'd done something with real and awful consequences.

Perhaps she'd just have to wait to tell him until it didn't matter, until he loved her so much that nothing she said would drive him away. And if it never got to that point, he'd walk away, none the wiser, and she'd be able to keep her awful secret.

As Gelsey looked through her childhood treasures, she heard a car pull up outside the cottage. She jumped off the bed and peered through the slit in the curtains to see Kellan striding up the garden walk. With a soft curse, she quickly restored the tin to its spot in the bedside table.

"Gels? Are you up?"

With another curse, she quickly pulled a T-shirt over her head and then stood beside the bed, carefully arranging the covers. Kellan walked in. "Hi," she said. "Just making the bed."

He grinned, then circled around and grabbed her waist before he pulled her down onto the bed. "Don't. We'll just mess it up again."

Gelsey smoothed her hand over his temple, brushing aside a lock of hair. "Why are you back here so soon?"

"I missed you," he said. He pulled her body against his. "I missed this. You've made it impossible to think about anything else."

"I find that hard to believe," she said, unable to hide a smile of satisfaction.

"It's true. No matter where I go, I'm thinking about your mouth…" He dropped a kiss on her lips. "And your shoulders…" He pulled aside the T-shirt and gently nibbled on the curve of her neck. "And your impossibly beautiful breasts." Kellan wriggled down until he could nuzzle the swell of flesh beneath her T-shirt.

"You're pathetic," Gelsey said, laughing.

"Yes. Yes, I am." He glanced up at her. "Actually, I came back here to get you. Jordan and Nan are helping with the painting and they insisted I bring you down. They're making a party of it."

Gelsey reached out for a pillow and brought it down on his head. "So you weren't thinking about my naked body? About the naughty things I did to you last night? About the words that you whispered in my ear while you were coming inside me?"

He frowned, then groaned softly. "I wasn't. But I am now."

She got up on her knees and pulled her T-shirt over her head. "So, what are you going to do about it?"

His gaze slowly skimmed over her body, as exciting as a caress. Gelsey felt a familiar knot of desire tighten inside her at the look in his eyes. It was so easy to make him want her. It didn't take much to have him hard and ready.

"Take off your clothes," she murmured.

As she watched him slowly undress, Gelsey thought of the young boy she'd first met on the cliffs. He was still there, in the twinkling blue eyes and finely sculpted mouth, in the boyish curl at his nape and the grin that made her weak in the knees.

This was fate. They belonged together. And nothing she could say or do would shake a bond that had survived so many years. She wanted to believe it was so. She needed to believe it.

"They're going to wonder where we are," Kellan whispered as he pulled her down onto the bed and settled himself above her.

Gelsey drew her legs up along his hips, her toes skimming along his calves. "I'm sure we can keep it under five minutes."

Kellan gasped, then braced himself on his elbows. "Five? Really? Why even bother, then?"

"Because five minutes in heaven is better than a day in the ordinary world." She drew him closer and then arched against him, his shaft pressing against her sex. Slowly, he pushed inside her, filling her with his heat.

"Don't move," she said.

"If I don't move, we'll be here all day."

"Five minutes." Gelsey pulled him close and kissed him, lingering for a long time over his mouth until she was sure he was properly distracted. And then, in a soft voice, she began to tell a story of man and mermaid, an erotic story of two people swept away by desire. She didn't leave out any detail, teasing him with a story of the seduction that had gone on between them from the moment they met.

His eyes were closed and Gelsey knew he was caught up in the images racing through his head. Her lips on his shaft, his teeth grazing her nipple. They didn't need to do it in order to experience it.

She shifted beneath him, just slightly, and his breath caught in his throat. But still, she wasn't ready for him to move. Every word she spoke was designed to bring him closer, to make his release come not from physical sensation, but from his imagination.

She sensed when he was close and then whispered in his ear. "Now you can move."

He drew back and then drove into her in an almost desperate search for pleasure. Again and again, she felt him deep inside her and then, in a single, silent instant, he was there, tumbling over the edge in a powerful orgasm.

When he was finally sated, he collapsed on the bed beside her, his leg thrown over her hips. "I stand corrected. I'm powerless against your rather considerable charms, my dear."

Gelsey smiled and dropped a kiss on his lips. "Five minutes."

"Good to know," he said. "Good for those times when we're waiting for the water to boil for tea or for football to come on the telly. Hell, it sometimes takes five minutes to get a pint at the pub. And there's a perfectly good closet just near the kitchen where we can—"

"Stop," Gelsey said. "We're only allowed to use the five-minute rule in emergencies." She sat up. "Come on, quick shower. And then we're going to go help with the painting."

"What about you? Should we take another five minutes for you?"

"You can take care of me in the shower," Gelsey said, jumping up from the bed. She grabbed his hands and pulled him to his feet, then wrapped his arms around her waist. But Kellan quickly turned her around in his arms, pressing his softening erection into the small of her back.

His hands smoothed down her belly to rest at the juncture of her thighs. He slipped a finger inside her, gently caressing her and before long, Gelsey felt her knees growing weak and her body surrendering to his touch.

His power over her body was just as startling as hers over his. She dissolved into deep soul-shattering spasms, grasping the bedpost to keep herself from collapsing. Breathless, she leaned back against him, wrapping her arm around his neck.

This had all begun with a simple kiss years ago. And yet, try as she might, she couldn't imagine a future without him, without this passion they shared. He had the power to give her incredible pleasure. But Kellan also had the power to break her heart into a million pieces.

KELLAN GLANCED OVER at the three men sitting at the end of the bar. Known as the Unholy Trinity, the trio of pensioners were regulars at the pub. Markus Finn, Dealy Carmichael and Johnnie O'Malley stopped by every day for a pint and a chat with whomever was available to listen to their brand of malarkey.

"What are you three gawkin' at?" Kellan asked from his spot at the opposite end of the bar. He'd been enjoying a quick beer while he waited for the takeaway lunch Riley had ordered for them all.

Markus leaned forward. "We hear you caught yourself a mermaid."

Kellan groaned. He couldn't go anywhere in town lately without having to answer questions about Gelsey. "She's not a mermaid," he said.

"How do ya know?" Dealy asked. "Have ya ever come 'cross a mermaid before?"

"No," Kellan said, trying to tamp down his irritation. "I just know. I've gotten a good look at her and there are no gills or scales or any such thing on her body."

"Of course not," Johnnie said. "There wouldn't be then. They disappear once she's on land."

"She's not a mermaid," Kellan insisted.

"I once saw a mermaid. Of course, I was three sheets to the wind, but it looked like a mermaid to me."

"Supposin' she was a mermaid," Markus said. "Just theoretically. Supposin' our little village of Ballykirk had its very own…what would we call it, lads?"

"Tourist attraction," Dealy said. "That's what you'd call it."

Markus stood and quickly moved to the stool beside Kellan. "Just hear us out, boyo, for it's an opportunity we'd be offerin'. You might already know that our little town got some money to help promote tourism and they made me head of the committee. And we've been looking for something that sets us apart from every other fishing village in Cork. And now we have it."

"You want to use Gelsey to bring tourists to Ballykirk?"

"In a word, yes!" Dealy said.

"You're crazy. She's not a mermaid," Kellan repeated.

"Well, I know that and you know that. Everyone in town knows that. But the tourists don't. That silly Blarney stone makes millions every year and we need a share of the money bein' thrown about. People come to Ireland because of the leprechauns and fairies and all those other silly legends."

"I realize that," Kellan said. "But I don't think Gelsey is interested in that kind of attention. She seems to be a woman who values her privacy."

"It's not like we'd be askin' her to swim around in a

giant tank all day," Markus said. "We just want to explore the marketing possibilities."

"Yeah," Dealy said. "The marketing possibilities."

"Do you have any idea what that means?" Kellan said.

Markus shrugged. "It was in the pamphlet the tourism board sent. But I know what I know. There's bleedin' leprechauns all over this island. But nobody has a mermaid." He shrugged. "You could mention it to her? See what she thought?"

"She has enough going on already. She took a job at Maeve's shop and—"

"She's workin' for Maeve?" Johnnie frowned. "Oh, Jaysus, that's not good. A few days with her and she'll be running as fast as she can from Ballykirk. The woman is mad as a hatter, that one."

"Not necessarily," Dealy said. "Maeve has been talking about selling her shop. We need to convince the mermaid to stay. What if we talk Maeve into selling the shop to Gelsey? A new retail establishment run by a clever little mermaid. The tourists will flock to Ballykirk."

"That's it," Markus said. "Now we have a plan." He clapped Kellan on the shoulder. "And just to make certain, we'd like you to hide the clothes you found her in. This whole scheme will go to hell if we lose her. I don't want to be takin' any risks."

"If you three start bothering her, she might decide to leave."

"Well, then, it's your job to keep her happy," Markus said. "She's…*community property.*"

"Maybe it is best that he talk to her about our scheme, boys," Johnnie said. "He's the one who rescued her. So she is beholden to him."

Dealy nodded, his expression serious. "Feel her out. Find out what she's lookin' for. She could make a real nice home for herself here in Ballykirk. And we could help her out. It would be mutually beneficial."

"Yeah," Markus said. "Tell her that. Mutually beneficial."

Katie appeared from the kitchen with their lunch order. She set the food in front of him, paper-wrapped sandwiches and bags of crisps tucked neatly into a box. Kellan drained the rest of the Guinness from his glass and pushed to his feet. He winked at Katie. "Thanks, love."

Katie grinned at him. "Bring your girl down to the pub for dinner so we can all get a look at her. We've got herring on the menu tonight. And Danny says she's a right vixen, she is."

"You, too?"

"Ah, I'm just playin' with you," Katie said. "Everyone is talking. We're all a bit curious about the girl."

Kellan headed to the door. Their offer was made. But Kellan was willing to consider anything that might keep Gelsey in Ballykirk. He didn't hold out much hope for her work at Maeve's—the woman had been a bit daft for as long as he could remember. But with Gelsey's beauty and charisma, it might just work.

Kellan recalled the phone conversation he'd heard the first night Gelsey had stayed with him. She had at least one person who cared enough to worry over her and maybe a place that she called home. But for some reason, she'd decided to stay in Ballykirk, at least for the near future.

Tucking the box under his arm, Kellan strode toward the waterfront. Riley and Nan had purchased a small cottage overlooking the harbor at Ballykirk. It was about the same size as the Quinn cottage on the hill, but it was in much worse condition. Riley had already replaced the roof and refinished the floors, but both the exterior and interior still needed painting and the windows were a mess.

Kellan had already contacted a few of the contractors who'd worked on Castle Cnoc and they'd agreed to do new plumbing and electricity at a bargain price. He'd decided it would be his wedding present to the happy couple.

When he arrived at the cottage, his brothers and the girls had decided to start work on the facade. The sun had warmed that side of the house and the breeze had died down, taking the last bit of chill out of the air.

"There he is," Riley called. "Poor Nan is about to faint from hunger."

Nan took a swipe at Riley with a paintbrush. "Hush."

Kellan glanced back and forth between the two of them, watching a pretty blush stain Nan's cheeks. "She's been working hard," he said. "She deserves a break for lunch."

"Oh, it's not that," Riley said.

"You said you were going to wait to tell them!" Nan cried.

"Tell us what?" Jordan asked. Danny and Gelsey joined the group with curious looks on their faces.

Riley slipped his arm around Nan's shoulders and grinned. "Nan is eating for two."

"Oh, don't worry about that," Jordan said. "I ordered two sandwiches, too. All of this outdoor work makes me so hungry."

"Don't mind her," Danny said. "All this fresh air has made her a bit cabbaged."

"What's cabbaged?" Gelsey whispered. "Why is she cabbaged? I ordered two sandwiches, too. Is that bad?"

"I expect this isn't about sandwiches. Riley is trying to tell us that Nan is going to have a baby," Kellan explained.

"Oh, my God," Jordan shouted. "Is that true?"

At Nan's nod, the entire group surrounded her for hugs and kisses. Even Gelsey offered her congratulations before stepping back to slip her arm through Kellan's. She looked over at him and smiled. "It's wonderful news."

"Yes." Kellan added, "Riley will make a fine father." He drew in a deep breath. The news had hit him in an odd way. He was happy for the couple, yet he felt a bit strange that Riley would experience fatherhood before he did. Kellan had always been the oldest boy, always been first at everything. But now, he seemed to be trailing behind in his brothers in all the important things.

"I'm going to fetch us a few more beers," he said, setting the box of sandwiches down on the front step.

"None for me," Nan said. "You can bring me a soda. I'm sorry, a mineral," she corrected, using the Irish word.

"You want to give me a hand?" Kellan asked Gelsey.

She followed him inside. The house was nearly empty, except for a few pieces of tatty furniture and the tools Riley was using to renovate the place. But there was a functioning refrigerator in the kitchen and it was stocked with cold drinks.

"Beer for me," Gelsey said.

He opened two bottles and handed one to her. "Are you having fun? Or is this too much too soon?"

"I like your brothers," Gelsey said, stepping across the kitchen to give him a kiss. She ran her hand along his cheek. "And I like Nan and Jordan, too."

"The two of them together can be a bit intimidating. They're both American and when they have an opinion they tend to just throw it out there for everyone to hear."

Gelsey shrugged. "I don't have many girlfriends," she murmured. "I think I'd like having a girlfriend if they were like Nan or Jordan."

Kellan leaned back against the refrigerator and watched a wistful expression dance across her pretty features. "You don't have any girlfriends?"

Gelsey shook her head. "No. Women usually don't like me."

"Why not?"

"Did you get me a corned-beef sandwich?" she asked, deftly changing the subject. "I love corned beef." Gelsey took the other beer from his hand, then headed for the door. By the time he joined her with the rest of the drinks, she was seated on the step, unwrapping her lunch. He gave his brothers each a beer and handed the mineral to Nan, before he sat down beside her.

Gelsey grabbed half the sandwich and bit into it, then groaned softly. "Oh, this is lovely. Are there any fries?"

Fries. Though he could detect a hint of an English accent in her speech, she sounded more like Nan and Jordan than any Brit he knew. But there was something else there. Occasionally, he caught her talking to herself in French or Spanish. "No chips, just crisps."

She looked at the bag. "Those are chips," she said.

"Ah, another little clue," Kellan said. "You reveal yourself a bit more every day. If you call crisps *chips* and chips *fries,* then you've spent time in the States."

"Very astute, Sherlock Holmes," she said. "My mother is American."

He leaned back and watched her eat, pondering the information she'd just revealed. It was the first real clue he had to who she was. "What about your father?"

"British," she said. "Interrogation over." She took a huge bite of her sandwich, then grinned at him.

Kellan chuckled at the funny face she made. For someone so slender, she certainly enjoyed a good meal now and then. She gobbled down her first corned-beef sandwich in just a few bites and then started on the second.

"Where do you come from?" Kellan asked.

She blinked as she looked at him, continuing to chew. "Come from?"

"You heard me. I don't get the accent. It's not Irish, I know that. It's not entirely American, either, or English. So what is it?"

She shrugged. "Lots of different things. A mash-up, really."

"Of what?" Kellan could see that she didn't want to reveal any more. But the woman was living in his house, eating food that he'd provided for her, socializing with his family. The least she could do was fill him in on a few details.

"Does it really make a difference?" she asked, watching him suspiciously.

"I'm just curious."

Her chin tilted up in defiance as she swallowed. "I spoke French as a child."

"You don't want me to know anything about you, do you? Why? What are you trying to hide? There's no reason. After a week together, we know each other about as intimately as we can."

She reached for a crisp and nibbled at it, considering her answer silently. "Can't we just leave it at that? We're both getting what we want out of this, so—"

"What *I* want? You're the one who crawled into bed with me that first night. I didn't invite you." Kellan cursed beneath his breath. "You know they're talking about you all around town. Markus Finn wants to capitalize on all this silly mermaid stuff. He thinks you could be like Ballykirk's very own Blarney Stone."

A gasp burst from her lips and then a giggle. Before long, she was laughing so hard, she had to set her sandwich down. "Really? But I'm not a mermaid." When she regained her composure, she drew a ragged breath and nodded. "Sorry. I didn't mean to laugh."

"The tourists wouldn't care," Kellan said. "They come to Ireland because of all the magic."

"So, what would I do?"

"He and the tourism committee are hoping you'll stay and maybe buy Maeve's shop from her. She's had it for sale for a few years now."

Gelsey crumpled the empty wrapper from her sandwich, then pulled her knees up to her chest, wrapping her arms around her legs. "I—I really don't know what my plans are," she said. "I'm not sure I could make a commitment like that right now."

"A commitment to Ballykirk or a commitment to me? You can tell me the truth."

"If I tell you the truth, you'll *want* me to leave," she countered. Gelsey raked her hands through her wavy hair, sighing softly as she tipped her head back. "I just need to have a moment to myself, a chance to take a breath without someone expecting something from me."

"Are you married?" Kellan asked.

"No!" Gelsey looked surprised. "No, there's no one. Not anymore."

"But there was?"

"It's over. Completely over. I swear to you."

A long silence grew between them. Gelsey reached out and took his hand, carefully lacing her fingers through his. "What difference does it make who we were?" she asked. "We began when you found me on the beach."

Kellan's gaze fell to her mouth, and without a second thought, he slipped his hand around her waist and pulled her into a long and languid kiss. She was right. He didn't care about anything beyond what they'd shared together. And though he knew she wasn't an amnesiac or a mermaid, that didn't matter, either. She was here with him now and that's all he cared about.

# 5

THE HILLS WERE SHROUDED in a dense mist as Gelsey navigated the battered Fiat toward Winterhill. She'd spent her last four or five Christmases skiing, surrounded by snow and plenty of twinkly lights. It was a bit odd to be staring out at fog.

Kellan had invited her to accompany him to Cork to pick up a set of plans he'd been waiting for and do a bit of Christmas shopping, but Gelsey had decided to take the morning for herself.

Everything was moving so fast in Ballykirk. Her feelings for Kellan were growing deeper with each day and night they spent together. And though he still questioned her about her past, he seemed to take her evasive answers with less frustration. So, had the time come to just be honest with him?

Their nights in bed were proof of his desire and their easygoing way with each other outside the bedroom marked a growing trust and friendship. But passion and friendship didn't necessarily add up to a future together. Gelsey had been through enough "relationships" to know how easily they fractured. And how quickly she grew bored.

She slowed the car as it neared a curve, sighing softly. How nice it would be to believe in love. To know that there was a man out there who could ensure complete happiness for the rest of her life. She'd been chasing that dream her entire life, but had never really believed it would come true.

At least she could make a real life for herself, a life with a job and a place to live, important things to occupy her day.

She'd stopped at the shop that morning, just to chat with Maeve about her job responsibilities. Though Gelsey couldn't offer any retail experience, she could offer enthusiasm and she saw incredible potential in the business that Maeve had started. When Maeve mentioned she was interested in selling the shop, the foundation of a new life had begun to take shape in her mind.

Why not make a life in Ballykirk? She could live at Winterhill and turn the shop into a thriving business. There was a huge market for unusual boutique skincare products, especially those made of natural ingredients. She knew women who paid thousands of dollars for a small jar of sheep placenta.

But until her problems in Italy were solved, until she faced the consequences of what she'd done, there could be no future for her in Ballykirk and no future with Kellan. The thought of jail, for something as silly as a punch in the face, was almost more than she could bear. She wasn't a criminal, but she'd done something that had broken the law.

Six months had passed and it still loomed over her like a big black cloud, obscuring any sunshine or hope she had. Antonio had been there and up until their fight, had promised to testify to what had happened. But now, she wasn't sure he'd hold up his end of the bargain.

The stone pillars flanking the driveway at Winter-hill appeared out of the fog. A feeling of relief washed over her at the sight of the old stone house. This was the only home she'd ever really known. Every summer, she'd arrived still dressed in her school uniform, ready to throw aside the rules and regulations for a summer full of fantasies.

Her grandmother had died six years ago, and since then, she hadn't been back. But three months ago, it had been the only place left to her, the only place in the world she could hide. Gelsey still expected her to be waiting at the door when she drove up to the house, her arms thrown wide and her eyes filled with tears of joy.

This would be a good place to start again, Gelsey mused. She could be happy here. She honked the horn, then smiled as the front door opened. Her grandmother's housekeeper came rushing out, her hands clutching her apron. Gelsey stepped out of the car only to be enveloped in Caroline's embrace.

"Oh, I should be livid, I should," Caroline said in her

thick Irish brogue. "Why haven't you phoned more than once? I've been worrying myself sick."

"I told you I was safe," she said.

"Safe? Look at this car you're drivin'! It's an accident waitin' to happen."

Gelsey looped her arm through Caroline's. "Come on, then. Let's have a cup of tea and I'll tell you all about my adventures in the real world."

"I'm not certain I want to hear," Caroline teased. "Are you driving without a permit?"

"No, I have a Spanish driver's license. I think it's good here."

"And where does that car come from?"

The housekeeper knew all of Gelsey's problems. Confession had been good for the soul and Gelsey had needed at least one person who understood what she'd done to her life. But no she couldn't wait to tell Caroline about her job and all the possibilities for her future in Ballykirk.

"Your mother and father have been calling," Caroline said. "They've been keeping up with the news on your case and they're worried."

"It's my problem," Gelsey said. "I'll deal with it."

Caroline gave her hand a squeeze as they walked to the front door. "Now, I want you to know that I haven't finished yet."

"Finished what?" Gelsey asked.

The housekeeper threw the door open and Gelsey stepped into the spacious foyer. "Christmas."

Gelsey gasped as she saw the beautiful pine garlands and twinkling lights. "Oh, look at this." Slowly, she took it all in, then stopped in front of a Christmas tree that sat just inside the parlor. It was decorated in an old-fashioned style, with faded blown-glass ornaments and tinsel and real candles on the tips of the boughs.

"Your grandmother used to insist that we do it up well," Caroline explained. "Christmas was her favorite day of the year, except for the day that you arrived at Winterhill for your summer holiday."

"I remember these," Gelsey said, reaching out to touch one of the candles. "I spent Christmas here one year when I was—"

"You were seven. I wasn't sure that you remembered."

"Oh, I do," Gelsey said. "It was magical."

"I thought, since you might be spending the holiday here again this year, I'd do it up, like your grandmother did." She gave Gelsey a quick hug. "Come, let's have tea. I want to hear all about this man you've met."

"Man? I didn't mention a man," Gelsey said.

"What else would have kept you away?"

Gelsey groaned as she walked back to the kitchen. "All right, there is a man. But it isn't want you think. At least, not entirely what you think."

She followed Caroline back to the kitchen, then sat down on one of the stools that surrounded the huge worktable in the center of the room. Cupping her chin in her hand, Gelsey watched as the housekeeper placed a plate of shortbread biscuits in front of her, then fussed with the preparations for tea. When the pot was filled and the tea steeping, she set it down on the table and joined Gelsey.

"Where have you been?"

"Ballykirk," Gelsey replied. "I've been staying with…with—a friend. His name is Kellan Quinn."

"Quinn? My cousin Aina married a Quinn from Ballykirk. Jamie Quinn."

"I haven't met him, though I'm sure there are a lot of Quinns in Ballykirk."

"Oh, they don't live in Ballykirk anymore. They moved to Galway years ago. I wouldn't think you'd have found Ballykirk very exciting."

"There's something in Ballykirk that I'm very interested in." Gelsey explained her hopes for Maeve's Potions and Lotions, describing the shop and Maeve's merchandise and the potential to turn the business into something special. When she finished, she looked at Caroline, waiting for her opinion.

"What is it?" Gelsey asked at the odd expression on the housekeeper's face. "I know it's silly to make plans with everything hanging over my head as it is. But I want to think positively. I need to believe that everything will work out."

"Oh, it's not that. You look…different." Caroline reached out and smoothed her hand over Gelsey's cheek.

"I do?"

Caroline nodded, her silver curls bobbing. "You look happy. Relaxed."

"I am," Gelsey said. "So do you think I should do it?"

"Let me ask you one question. How much of your interest in staying in Ireland has to do with this Quinn bloke?"

"I suppose some," Gelsey admitted. "But I'm not really counting on that for the future. I think it's time I begin to plan my life for myself and not whatever man I happen to fancy at the moment."

"Antonio has been ringing here, trying to get in touch. It sounds like he's very sorry for what he did and he wants to make amends."

"Of course he's sorry. All men who cheat are sorry. And I suppose I shouldn't blame him. I ran away to Ireland and he needed someone. In his case, anyone would do."

"He wasn't ever right for you, Gelsey."

She drew a deep breath and nodded. "I know. But after the fight we had, I'm not sure he's going to want to testify for me in court. He was there when it happened. He saw the whole thing."

"Perhaps you should try to smooth things out," Caroline suggested. "For the sake of your future."

Gelsey shook her head. "I'm done with Antonio," she said. "And that life. I want to start a new life, here at Winterhill."

Caroline took her hands and gave them a squeeze. She stared down at Gelsey's ring finger. "Where is your engagement ring?"

"I threw it in the ocean," Gelsey said.

"That was a foolish thing to do."

"I suppose I should have kept it. I could have traded it for all the things I left at his villa in Portugal."

"That would have been the sensible thing."

"Agreeing to marry a Spanish race-car driver with an ex-wife, an ex-mistress and a girlfriend on the side was not sensible. From now on, I'm going to make myself happy first." She paused, then grinned. "Not that I'm giving up men entirely."

"Well, I think that's a grand plan," Caroline said. "Just grand. I have always thought that you deserved more happiness than you allowed yourself." Caroline's eyebrows arched. "Now tell me more about this man."

Gelsey laughed. "He's very sweet and far too serious for me. And, even though I'm afraid I'll find some way to muck it all up, he makes me feel…safe." She shook her head. "I've spent my life living dangerously and now I'm happy with a cozy cottage and handsome architect in my bed. How strange is that?"

"You haven't had an easy time of it, Gelsey. I've been witness to that. But it would fulfill your grandmother's fondest wish if you could find some happiness here."

Gelsey drew a ragged breath, then smiled. "I love this house. Maybe that's why I came running here when things with Antonio fell apart."

"Well, I'll make sure everything is just so for you," Caroline said.

"And I'm going to help this year."

"You're going to come back, then?"

Gelsey thought about it for a long moment, then nodded. "Yes. And I'm going to bring Kellan with me. Just as soon as I tell him who I really am."

"Just who does he think you are?" Caroline asked.

Gelsey winced, then shrugged her shoulders. "At first, a mermaid. But now, probably an escapee from a mental hospital."

"Oh, dear," Caroline said. "It's going to take more than a pot of tea to explain that."

"WHAT THE HELL are we doing here?" Danny grumbled.

"Waiting," Kellan said.

"I can see that. What are we waiting for?"

"I'm not sure."

"When you asked to borrow my car, you told me you had an errand to run. We're not running. We're sitting here at the side of the road staring at a huge house. Who lives there?"

"I don't know," Kellan muttered. "Do you?"

Danny shook his head. "Not really. I'm not sure anyone lives there, at least not year-round. But it looks like a nice place. Well tended. The ironwork on the gates looks original. I'd like to get a closer look at those hinges." He reached for the door handle, but Kellan grabbed his jacket sleeve.

"Wait," he said. "Look. There's someone coming outside. Pull ahead and then turn around."

"Who's coming?" Danny asked.

"I don't know. Someone that Gelsey knows. She came here this morning. Drove the Fiat over. I couldn't stick around because she would have recognized my car, so I decided to come back and check it out once she returned to Ballykirk."

"You followed her here?"

"Not exactly," Kellan said. Then he cleared his throat. "Well, yeah, I did. I was driving back to the cottage to try to convince her to go to Cork with me after Jordan canceled. And I saw her turn down the coast road, so I followed her—at a discreet distance. I was curious. And this is where she came. To this house."

"What kind of sick obsession is this?" Danny said.

"I was beginning to think she *was* a feckin' mermaid. I'm losing my mind, here. She won't tell me anything about herself. I decided to find out on my own. Now I just have to figure out why she came here."

"Maybe it's where she lives?"

"If she lives here, why is she staying in the cottage with me? This place looks a lot more posh than anything I can offer. Look at the bleedin' chimneys. There must be five or six fireplaces in that house."

"Look, a woman's come out," Danny said. "She's putting a wreath up on the door. I'm going to go talk to her."

"No!"

"I'll just tell her I'd like to take a photo of her gates. I do it all the time."

Danny hopped out of the Land Rover and started off toward the woman, leaving Kellan no choice but to follow him.

"Hello, there!" Danny called, striding confidently

up the driveway. "We were just looking at your gate. I'm a blacksmith. Would you mind if I took a photo?" He glanced back at Kellan and motioned him forward. "Do you have your mobile with you?"

Kellan reached into his pocket, then handed Danny his phone. "Just flip it open and press that button on the side. Then press it again to take the photo."

"Would you mind?" Danny asked again.

"No, not at all," the old woman said.

"How long have you owned the place?" Danny asked.

"Oh, I don't own it. I work here. I'm the housekeeper. For thirty-five years. My mother worked here before me."

"Big house," Danny said. "A lot to keep up with, I'd reckon."

"Oh, it's not all that bad. The owner only comes now and then. She's here now, so I've been a bit busier."

"She?" Kellan asked.

"Yes. Miss Gelsey. I've know her since she was just a wee baby."

"Really."

"Her grandmother owned the house up until the time she died. That was six years ago. She was Lila Dunleavy Woodson. Her husband was a surgeon in London and they kept a summer home here. Her son, Gelsey's father, became a diplomat with the British Foreign Service and married an American." She chuckled. "You wouldn't need to know all that genealogy just to look at a gate, now, would you?"

"I guess not," Danny said. "I'll just get a few snaps and we'll be on our way.

By the time they got back in the car, Kellan's mind was spinning. Woodson. Her name was Gelsey Woodson. She had parents and a home—a very lovely home from the look of it. And she had a housekeeper. She'd obviously come home to pick up the expensive clothes, expensive clothes that had magically appeared in the wardrobe sometime before lunch.

Kellan stared out the window, watching as the scenery passed by. "What the hell am I doing?"

"You are definitely in love with this girl," Danny said. "I've never seen you so out of joint over a woman." He gave Kellan a sideways glance. "She did seem a bit more posh than the average girl. She has good manners. Jordan even mentioned that the other day. Nan thought she might be a ballerina because she has such nice posture, but Jordan guessed fashion model. I figured she was rich from the way she talked."

"I don't even know why I'm interested," Kellan said.

"Because she's drop-dead gorgeous. Hell, Kellan, you'd be an eejit if you walked away from a goddess like her." Danny pointed up the road. "Are you coming into town with me or should I drop you at the cottage?"

"Let's go to the pub," he said. "I think I could use a pint or two. And I left my car there."

When they arrived at the pub, they found a crowd inside, oddly large for a Monday afternoon. But as

Kellan stared at the group clustered around the bar, he suddenly realized why they had all come.

"Looks like your mermaid is holding court," Danny said.

Gelsey was perched on a bar stool with the Unholy Trinity lined up to her left. Doc Finnerty occupied the stool to her right and a small group of townspeople filled out the rest of her circle.

Kellan strolled to the end of the bar to greet his mother. "How long has she been here?"

"About an hour," his mother said. "Where have you boys been?"

"I've been draggin' Kellan around the countryside looking for leprechauns," Danny said with an exaggerated Irish brogue.

Frowning, Kellan watched as Dealy and Markus commandeered the conversation. If they were bothering Gelsey with their plans, he was going to put an end to it right now. He pushed away from the end of the bar and strode through the small crowd to stand in front of Gelsey.

Reaching up, she threw her arms around his neck and gave him a quick kiss. "You're back," she said. "I came in here looking for you, but your mother said you and Danny had left together."

"I thought I'd find you at the cottage."

"I walked into town to talk to Maeve, then decided to stop here after. Then these gentlemen came by. They said you sent them."

Kellan glared at the trio over Gelsey's shoulder.

"They did, did they? Well, that's interesting. As I recall, I haven't spoken to them since the day before yesterday when I told them to keep their silly plans to themselves."

Gelsey glanced back at Johnnie, Markus and Dealy. "But they've been wonderful," she said. "They thought I might be interested in a business opportunity and I told them I was."

"You don't need to listen to these gits," Kellan whispered.

"Really," Gelsey said. "It's an interesting plan. One I've actually been considering." She grabbed Kellan around the arm and pulled him along with her toward the door. "It was a pleasure meeting all of you and I'm sure I'll see you again soon. And thank you for the beer, Mrs. Quinn."

"No trouble," Maggie Quinn called, a satisfied grin on her face. "Come back soon, Gelsey."

When they got outside, Kellan drew her along to his car, parked just a few steps from the front door of the pub. He opened the passenger side. "Get in," he muttered.

Gelsey hopped inside and a few moments later, Kellan got behind the wheel, gripping it with white-knuckled hands. "Gelsey, I don't want you perpetrating this mermaid stuff anymore. It might have been fun at first, but it will only make things difficult for you."

"I wasn't," she said. "And it's just silliness. No one really believes I'm a mermaid. Why are you so angry?"

Kellan's jaw twitched. That was a good question.

He'd become so protective of Gelsey, yet he couldn't figure out his motives. He cared about her, yet he'd been very careful about letting himself feel too much. He enjoyed her company and didn't want anyone or anything interfering with that. And he sensed that she was searching for something, something she'd never be able to find in Ballykirk.

"It is an intriguing opportunity," she said. "And with the proper marketing, it might bring more tourists into Ballykirk. The mermaid thing would just be a…what did Dealy call it…a hook, to get people interested."

Kellan glanced over at her. "I thought you couldn't commit to something like that. Isn't that what you said?"

Gelsey nodded. "Yes. But I have to make a life for myself somewhere. Why not here?" She swallowed, forcing a smile. "Unless, of course, you don't want me to. You can tell me, if that's the case. I'm perfectly fine with that. And don't think that, just because I buy the shop, I expect us to continue a relationship. I know what we have might not be…"

"What do we have?" Kellan asked.

"You know."

"No, I'm not sure I do. At least, I'm not sure what you think we have. What would you call it?"

She thought about her answer for a long moment. "Did you ever see the film *Roman Holiday,* with Audrey Hepburn and Gregory Peck?"

Kellan shook his head. What was this about?

"It's about these two people who know that being

together is probably impossible, but they spend a wonderful two days together in Rome. She was a princess and I'm not. And they never had sex. And we've been together a lot longer than two days, but..." She cursed softly. "It's the idea of it. We can still be great together even if it isn't meant to last forever. Does that make sense?"

Kellan frowned. "It might make better sense if I watched the movie."

"Well, maybe we should find a place to rent it and we can watch it tonight. It will all make sense then."

The only thing that would make sense to Kellan would be a complete explanation of who she was and what she was really doing in Ballykirk. And if it took watching some silly chick flick to get her to talk about herself, then he was prepared to do that.

"Our library has a decent collection of DVDs," Kellan said. "Maybe we can find it there."

"THIS IS NOT ANYTHING like *Roman Holiday*," Gelsey said. She was curled up against Kellan's body, her gaze fixed on the laptop that rested on his belly. She reached for the popcorn bowl and grabbed a handful, then slowly munched. "This has cowboys and covered wagons. *Roman Holiday* has ancient ruins and Vespas."

"The library didn't have *Roman Holiday*. But Gregory Peck is in this one."

*"How the West Was Won,"* Gelsey said. "Couldn't we have at least gotten a romance? Or a Christmas film?

*It's a Wonderful Life* or *How the Grinch Stole Christmas.*"

"I like this one," Kellan said. He glanced over at her, then reached for the computer and closed the top. "All right, we probably could have done better for our first movie night."

"Next time, I get to pick," she said.

It was odd how something as simple as movie night was so satisfying. For so many years, her idea of an exciting evening involved an expensive dress, an even more expensive bottle of champagne and a nightclub filled with handsome men. Tonight was just one man and a movie and it was perfect—except for the movie.

Kellan leaned over and kissed her, his tongue tracing the shape of her mouth. "Next time, you can choose." He set the computer on the floor, then crawled beneath the bedcovers. Gelsey stretched out beside him, slipping into the curve of his arm, her head resting on his shoulder.

"I had a really good day today," she murmured.

"Yes?"

"Yes. And I think tomorrow is going to be even better." She glanced up at him. "I get to start work tomorrow. I have a real job and I'm going to be gainfully employed."

"Not everyone is so excited to go to work," he said. "Are you really serious about buying her shop?"

"Maeve would sell me all her recipes," Gelsey said. "And we would manufacture them at the shop to start. We'd have to update the jars and the labels. I know they'd sell at five times the price, especially in some of the exclusive shops in Europe." She paused. "I have a lot of ideas."

"So, you'll look for investors?"

She shook her head. "No. I won't need investors."

"How will you pay for it?"

"I'll figure that out," she murmured. It was an awfully big hole in her plan, at least from his point of view. "I have a little money of my own."

Kellan cursed softly, then tossed the bedcovers aside and got out of bed. He grabbed his jeans from the floor and pulled them on. "I could really use a walk. I'll be back in a bit."

His sudden change of mood stunned her at first. But then she realized that this was bound to happen sooner or later. "I'll come with you," she said.

"No, I need some time to myself."

"You're angry."

Kellan gritted his teeth, then shook his head. "What kind of game is this?" he asked. "And why the hell have you decided to play it with me?"

"I—I don't know what you mean," Gelsey said, avoiding his gaze. She knew exactly what he meant, but she wasn't sure she wanted to admit that.

"I don't know who the hell you are," he said, pacing back and forth at the end of the bed. "We share the most intimate things and yet, I don't know anything about you."

"What's wrong with that? What difference does it

make? The past is in the past. Why are you so determined to dredge it all up?"

God, he was so beautiful when he was angry. Kellan was always so controlled, so sure of himself. She wanted him to crawl back into bed and make love to her, to turn all that anger he felt into passion.

"And why are you so determined to hide it? You're playing a dangerous game here, Gelsey."

"I'm not afraid," she retorted.

Kellan drew a long, deep breath, then shrugged. "Well, maybe I am. How the hell am I supposed to figure this all out if I don't have any of the facts?"

"What do you need to figure out?" she asked. "Can't you just be happy living in the moment?"

"No," Kellan said. "That's not who I am. I'm a thinker and a planner and an organizer. I don't like… ambiguity."

"Not everything is worth knowing."

"You think this is some game? Well, I don't want to play anymore. It's over. The clock's run out. And I think it's time you told me."

Gelsey felt her anger rise. She didn't owe him any explanations. She shouldn't be forced to admit all the mistakes she'd made in her life, especially not to a man she'd only known for a week. "What do you want me to say? I'm married. I'm engaged. I've slept with hundreds, no, thousands of men. I've danced naked for strangers…and money. I've tried every illicit drug known to mankind. And I'm really a man trapped in a woman's body."

"Is any of that true?" Kellan asked.

"No. Aren't you glad it isn't? The truth is much less interesting. And if you really cared about me, it wouldn't matter."

He circled the bed and sat down beside her. "You're afraid," he said. "You're afraid that I'll find something about you that I don't like."

"No," Gelsey said. "I just don't care about who you were before we met. That part of your life didn't involve me. Our lives began that morning on the beach. We're like…goldfish."

"Goldfish?"

"They live completely in the moment. If you watch a fish in a bowl, by the time he gets across the bowl, he's forgotten where he was. It doesn't matter to him."

"That's bollocks," Kellan muttered. "I don't live like a feckin' fish. I'm willing to take the good with the bad. If we don't start to be honest with each other, then we don't have any chance to make this work."

"You want to make this work? What does that mean? It already works. If you try any harder, you might wreck it."

"Maybe so. But this is it, Gelsey. This is the deal breaker. I need some answers."

She considered his demand for a long moment, then nodded. "Have you ever played the game Twenty Questions? It's a game I used to play with my nanny."

"You had a nanny?" Kellan asked.

"Yes. Her name was Marie and she was French. She's the one who taught me how to speak French. My mother thought it was important. That's one question. And I'm only giving you five. So you have four left."

"What's your name?" Kellan asked.

"I'm Gelsey Evangeline Woodson. I'm named after my mother's favorite ballet dancer and my father's favorite poem."

"Where are your parents?"

"I have no idea," Gelsey said. "My mother is probably in New York. And the last time I heard, my father was in Hong Kong. We don't really communicate. They have their lives and I have mine." She sent him a sideways glance. "See. Some of the answers aren't very pretty. My parents divorced when I was eight and sent me off to boarding school. I used to come to Ireland every summer to stay with my grandmother at Winterhill, her house."

"Boarding school?"

"Yes. And that's four. In Switzerland. It's as awful as it sounds. I was lonely and homesick and I had trouble making friends. Last question."

Kellan considered his options silently. "I think I'll save my last question," he said.

"You can't. It's against the rules. You have to ask me now or lose the question."

"This game has rules?" Kellan chuckled. "Doesn't that go against the whole 'living for the moment' thing? Why not seven questions? Or eleven? Who cares how many questions were asked in the past? I say that we should play with forty-six questions. Just to live in the moment."

"Ask your last question," she said, bristling at the sarcasm in his voice. "Or don't." Gelsey crawled out of bed and picked up her clothes from the floor. She tugged on her shirt without putting on a bra, then pulled on her jeans. "I think I'm going to go."

"Go where?"

"Home," she said. "And that's your last question." She brushed past him. She found her boots at the door and slipped her bare feet inside, then put on her jacket. But by the time she opened the door, Kellan was beside her, pushing it shut again.

"Don't go," he murmured.

"I don't want to do this. I don't want to fight with you." This was all so familiar, she mused. It had happened with every man she'd ever known. Accusations, recriminations. Why did every man have to dwell in the past?

"I'm sorry. It's just difficult for me."

"Why? It's so easy. We know how we feel, right now, in the moment. And in a few minutes, it will all be forgotten."

"Is that the way it works? You'll forget that I've been a bloody caffler?"

"I don't even know what that is," Gelsey said.

"An arse of the highest order. An eejit. A proper prick."

She smiled. "Yes, I believe the description suits you quite well."

He slipped his arms around her waist and kissed her, lingering over her mouth until she parted her lips. The kiss was perfectly executed to make her forget the argument they'd just had and by the end of it, Gelsey was convinced.

"Stay with me," he murmured. "I don't want you to go."

"If I stay, no more questions."

"No more questions."

"All right. I'll stay."

Kellan picked her up and wrapped her legs around his waist, then carried her into the bedroom. "Gelsey Evangeline Woodson," he murmured, kissing her neck. "I like that."

"My friends used to call me Gigi," she said. "But I hate that name now."

"I like Gels," he said. "Will that do?"

# 6

KELLAN STRODE INTO the Hound, searching the dimly lit interior as he walked to the bar. Overnight, the place had been decorated for the holidays with twinkling garlands draped from every spot possible and a Christmas tree sitting in the corner.

But there was something a bit nicer about it all, he mused as he took it all in, he could see Jordan and Nan's influence on the family business already. Kellan recognized his brother's Christmas CD playing over the sound system.

Riley was washing glasses and nodded at him as he approached. "Big brother, what are you about on this fine day?"

"The place looks grand," Kellan said. "Very festive. But the music is crap."

Riley chuckled. "Thanks. I'll let the management know."

"Have you seen Gelsey? I stopped up at the cottage to pick her up and she wasn't there."

"She's over at the church. The ladies' guild is meeting this afternoon and they asked if she might come and speak to them."

"About what?"

"I guess what it's like to be a mermaid?"

Kellan ground his teeth. "If I hear that mermaid shite once more, I swear, I'm going to pummel someone. It's not funny anymore."

"She's over there demonstrating something…something to do with kelp?" Riley chuckled. "I find it quite amusing that she gets you so riled up. I have precious little entertainment here in Ballykirk, but you've been providing more than enough these past couple of weeks."

"How would you feel if Nan went about telling everyone she'd once been a seal?"

Riley thought about that for a moment, then shrugged. "I see your point. But, hell, if it sold more Guinness at the pub, I'd be all for it. Who cares what a bunch of tourists believe? And I hear that business is booming at Maeve's and she's only been working there a week. Five customers yesterday. That's more than Maeve used to have in a month."

"Well, the ladies' guild isn't a bunch of tourists." Kellan pushed away from the bar and walked back outside, then headed toward the church, all the while thinking about what he was going to say to her. She'd told him the truth a week ago. He knew where she was from and how she grew up. He'd just assumed that the mermaid stories were finally going to stop, at least to the locals.

The ladies were gathered in the meeting room of the church. Kellan threw open the doors only to be greeted by surprised silence and twenty or thirty pairs of inquisitive eyes.

"Perfect!" Gelsey said. "You're right on time." She hurried up to Kellan and grabbed his arm, pulling him into the room. "Now, ladies, as I was saying, all these products work just as well on men as they do on women. Many of your men are exposed to the elements every day in their work world and the skin can become wrinkled and leathery. It's no good walking around town with a man who looks as if he's twice your age, right?"

This brought a chorus of approval from the women. Gelsey shoved Kellan into a chair. "What are you doing here?" he murmured.

"A product demonstration," she whispered. "If they won't come to the shop, then the shop will go to them." She turned back to the audience. "Now, the first thing we'll begin with is this sea-salt exfoliator. We just apply this all over the face, with gentle fingers, avoiding the eyes, nostrils and mouth, of course." She looked down at Kellan. "Tip your head back. You'll like this."

"You're not going to put that on my face," he muttered.

"Of course, Kellan, being the typical male, will probably resist. But it's your job, ladies, to make this a pleasant experience. Put on some soft music, maybe

dress a bit provocatively. And get close. Get very close."
She stepped over his lap, her legs on either side of his.

"You'll like this," she whispered. "I promise."

Reluctantly, Kellan closed his eyes. Slowly, she began to massage the gritty cream into his face, her fingers dancing over his skin and smoothing across his forehead. After only a few seconds, he found himself relaxing, enjoying the touch of her hands.

"This really can be quite sensual, ladies. So, I'd suggest that you reserve this treatment for a time when the two of you can truly appreciate all the benefits."

Kellan tried to keep his pulse from racing, but it was no use. Thankfully, the front of his jacket would cover any unexpected reaction, although from the way Gelsey was talking, that's exactly what she was looking for.

"Now, I have some lovely samples for all of you in these little gift bags and I want you all to try them on yourself and on your man. I've also included a sprig of mistletoe. I'm sure you know what to do with that. Remember, all our products are one hundred percent natural. No artificial colors or scents."

Kellan tried to look at her, but a tiny bit of salt dropped off his lashes, burning his eye. "Gels," he murmured. "I think it's time to get this off." But from what he could hear, Gelsey had wandered off to talk to some of her potential customers and forgotten all about him. Kellan got to his feet and blindly searched for a towel to wipe his face. He banged into a table, then nearly tripped over a chair before he felt Gelsey's hand on his arm.

"Come on, then," she said. "Sit down and I'll finish your treatment."

"Don't you dare," he warned. "You're not going to seduce me in the parish meeting room."

"I meant your facial treatment. It doesn't always have to come with sex, you know." She gently wiped the salt mixture from his face and he opened his eyes. "There you are," she murmured. "Handsome as ever." She bent closer and brushed a kiss across his lips.

Kellan slipped his arms around her waist. "Did you really need to put that stuff on my face?"

"I'm selling product," she said. "If I'm going to take over Maeve's store, I'm going to need to get out and stir up some business, especially from the ladies in the area. Regular customers are important. I've already lined up a presentation with the ladies' group over in Glengarriff. Mrs. Murphy's sister is on the program committee and they're always looking for speakers. It would help if you'd come with me."

"You don't need me," he said. "I saw how you were with the ladies. You're good at this, Gelsey. People like you."

"You really think so? You think I'm good?"

Kellan nodded. The simple compliment brought a beautiful joy to her face. That's all it took for him, he thought. As long as she was happy, so was he. Simple, but now he was beginning to understand her approach to life. Dwelling in the past only made the present miserable. She'd forgotten their argument minutes after it had happened and hadn't brought it up since.

"I'm not sure what my schedule is going to be like after the first of the year," he said. "I've got to go back to work soon."

"Where?"

"We bid on a museum project in France. In Brittany. I'm not sure we're going to get it and—"

"You're going to France? For how long?"

"We don't have the job yet," Kellan said. In truth, he wasn't sure he wanted it anymore. Gelsey was here, in Ballykirk. And her plans to buy Maeve's shop would keep her here. France was a long way from Ireland.

He'd been thinking a lot about business. He had some savings and contacts with good investors. Maybe it was time to take that risk, to put his own cash behind a project and reap the profits. After all, Gelsey was used to a comfortable lifestyle. And he couldn't really offer her as much doing just design and engineering on a project. He needed to make some real money.

"Don't worry," he said. "It will work itself out." But as he reassured her, Kellan knew that it wouldn't be so simple. He'd become accustomed to coming and going as he pleased, without a thought to anyone else's feelings. If he and Gelsey were together, then all of that would change. His whole life would change.

He watched as Gelsey packed her boxes and collected her papers. Already, he could see the changes in her. She was confident, so different from the nervous woman he'd sent off to her first day at work just a week ago. In truth, she seemed completely in her element.

"Can I buy you lunch?" he asked.

"I'm going to buy you lunch," she said, waving a stack of cards at him. "I made over a hundred pounds in sales today."

"You don't have to do that," he said.

"No, I want to. Maeve gave me an advance on my pay and I have just enough to buy you lunch. She's been very pleased with my work. That's important. I'm not sure she'd sell to someone who wasn't passionate about the business."

Kellan helped her carry the boxes out to the battered Fiat. "You're going to have to get yourself a better car," he said.

"I know. I've never had a car of my own. But there is a car at Winterhill. I'm not sure it runs anymore. It belonged to my grandmother."

"You could get it fixed," he said. "I could help you out with that."

Gelsey opened the back hatch of the Fiat and put the box she carried inside. Kellan dropped his box next to the first and shut the hatch. But the catch didn't always work and it took three tries before the hatch stayed closed. "Yeah, you definitely need a better car."

She slipped her arms around his neck and kissed him. "Have I told you what a good man you are?"

"I believe you have," Kellan said. "Usually in bed. I think this might be the first time outside the bedroom."

"I've never said that in the bedroom."

"Not in those exact words," he said.

"What words did I use?"

"Little words," Kellan teased. "Like…*oh* and…*yes*.

And then sometimes you say my name over and over. I may be wrong, but I assumed you were telling me I was a good man."

Gelsey laughed. "You assumed right. But I think I need to say it out loud more often." She tipped her face up to the sun. "Kellan Quinn is a very good man," she shouted.

"He's a feckin' gobshite."

The voice came from the direction of Danny's smithy and Kellan shrugged. "I guess we have other opinions on the subject."

"That's because they've never spent a night in bed with you," Gelsey replied.

"Actually, my brothers and I used to share a bed when we were little."

"You know what I mean," Gelsey said.

"I know exactly what you mean."

THE LATE-AFTERNOON SUN shone through the plate-glass windows of Maeve Dunphrey's shop, illuminating dust motes with every movement that Gelsey made. She pushed up on her tiptoes to grab a box from the top shelf of the old wooden wall displays, then carefully made her way down the wobbly ladder.

"Some of this stuff has to be forty years old," she said, setting the box on the counter in front of her. "I suppose we should try to salvage some of these jars. They're so pretty and, technically, they are vintage."

Jordan walked over and pulled a jar of lavender-scented lotion from the box. She screwed off the top and gave in a sniff before wrinkling her nose. "Yeah, this is pretty far gone. But the jar is lovely."

"I can go see if they have an old bucket at the Hound," Nan offered. "We can dump the stuff in there and then put the jars through the pub's dishwasher."

Gelsey nodded, grateful for the help that Nan and Jordan had offered. She'd spent a fair bit of her first week of work just cleaning, going through boxes and crates, discarding old inventory and taking stock of what was available in the store. When Nan and Jordan had stopped by a few days ago, they'd offered to help and had returned every afternoon since, making the job much more pleasant.

Nan stood in the center of the sales floor, her hands hitched on her waist, and surveyed the nearly tidy shop. "It's actually starting to look good," she said. "All these old wooden cases look beautiful, once you can see them."

"Thank you so much for helping out," Gelsey said. "You girls really didn't need to do this."

"You helped paint my house," Nan said.

"And hopefully, you'll be around when I have some tedious chore to do," Jordan added. "Are you really thinking of buying this place?"

Gelsey nodded. "Yes. I think I could make a success of it. There's a little shop like this on the Rue des Arts in Paris and women flock to it. They send their empty jars from all over the world to get them refilled. I bought night cream from them all the time, even when I was living in Portugal with Antonio."

Nan and Jordan glanced at each other. "You lived in Portugal?"

Gelsey blinked, surprised that she had been so honest with them. Over the past few days, they'd become good friends and she hadn't thought to continue the pretense. And now, in a single unguarded moment, she'd given it all away. "That was a lifetime ago." She laughed softly, shaking her head. "It's beautiful there. Very…sunny. Much like Spain. I lived there for a time, too."

Nan glanced at Jordan again, then looked back at Gelsey. "We know about Portugal. And Antonio. We've sort of known the truth from early on."

"You did?"

Jordan walked over to the counter and retrieved her purse then rummaged through it. A few moments later, she pulled out a magazine clipping and handed it to Gelsey. "I came across that while I was waiting to get my hair cut in Glengarriff. It's from *Hello!* magazine from a year ago."

The picture wasn't one of her best, Gelsey thought as she examined it closely. She was wearing a designer dress that barely covered her ass, an ass that was quite visible in the photo. A champagne bottle dangled from one hand and a cigarette from the other. "I was so drunk, I don't remember anyone taking this photo," she murmured, handing it back to Jordan. "It doesn't even look like me."

"You're Gigi Woodson," Nan said.

"I *was* Gigi Woodson."

Jordan crumpled up the clipping and tossed it into a nearby rubbish bin. "Does Kellan know?"

Gelsey winced. "No. But I'm pretty sure he's about to find out."

"We're not going to say a word," Jordan said. "We promise."

"If you know about Antonio, then I'm sure you know about the incident with the Italian photographer?"

Nan shook her head. "No. And you don't have to tell us. We really don't need to know."

"Thank you," Gelsey said. "I suppose I should be glad I managed to get away with it for this long. I assumed someone would recognize me sooner or later." She raked her hand through her hair, then forced a smile. "I guess I haven't changed all that much."

"You look completely different," Jordan disagreed.

"Completely," Nan added.

"I felt like I recognized you when we met," Jordan continued, "but I couldn't figure out where it had been. And when I saw the photo in *Hello!*, it just clicked."

Suddenly, a rush of emotion overwhelmed Gelsey. She fought back tears as she picked up the crumpled clipping. "You can show him," she murmured, holding it out to Nan. "I—I don't care. It really shouldn't make a difference." Gelsey felt a hand on her back and she found Jordan standing behind her. "I just really wanted to start over."

"We're not going to say anything," Jordan said.

"Not even to Danny and Riley?" Gelsey asked.

Nan laughed. "Are you kidding? Those two are horrible at keeping secrets. But to be honest, I don't think it's such a big deal. Kellan loves you. He won't care."

"He doesn't love me," Gelsey said. "And you've only seen one photo. There are hundreds out there. And none of them make me look very good. At least, not to a guy like Kellan." A tear trickled down her cheek and she brushed it away, embarrassed by her show of emotion. Drawing a ragged breath, she forced a smile. "I think we should call it a day. It's nearly four and you two have your own things to do."

Nan patted Gelsey on the shoulder, then thought better of it and gave her a clumsy hug. "It will all work itself out," she said. "You'll see."

Jordan gave her a hug, as well. "Kellan is a good guy. He wouldn't let something like this change his feelings for you."

The girls grabbed their jackets and purses and headed out the front door. Gelsey waved to them as they passed by the windows, going toward the pub. She had at least a few more hours of work ahead of her, but it was better to pass that time on her own, rather that be faced with more explanations.

Maybe Nan and Jordan were right. Maybe her past wouldn't make any difference to Kellan. At least at first. But once everyone else knew, once the press figured out where she was, Gelsey couldn't guarantee that he'd feel the same way.

She'd fought a five-year battle with the paparazzi and in most of the skirmishes, she'd lost badly. In the end, Gigi Woodson sold papers and that was all that mattered. They'd followed her through two broken engagements, a stint in rehab and a very ill-conceived six-day marriage to an already married Argentinean polo player. The end of her third engagement had sent her running back to Winterhill, out of sight and hopefully out of mind.

She was startled out of her thoughts by the sound of her mobile. Gelsey found it sitting on the counter next to the cash register and glanced at the screen. Her stomach twisted into a knot as she recognized the name of her attorney in Rome. She set the phone down, not ready to deal with whatever he had to tell her. She'd call him back later.

The bell above the door jingled and Gelsey spun around to see Kellan standing at the front of the shop, a surprised expression on his handsome face. "Bloody hell, look at this place. You've done wonders."

Gelsey felt her spirits brighten. "I know. Not alone though. Nan and Jordan have been helping out a lot. We've almost got all the old inventory cleared away. Next week, I can start to do a little decorating. Jordan has already given me some great ideas. And Nan thinks we ought to carry some books and CDs, too. Kind of a whole holistic approach."

"Sounds grand to me." Kellan walked toward her, then slipped his arms around her waist. "Nan and Jordan are back at the pub. I thought you might like to join us there. The family is getting together for dinner. My sister Shanna and her husband and kids came down from Dublin and they're staying the night.

It's my niece's birthday. Lily. She's five. And my sister Claire will be here with her kids. I'd like you to meet them all."

"Really?"

Kellan nodded. "Yeah. You've met the rest of the family, why not them?"

"I—I really should stay here and get some more done. We have a sale starting and tomorrow the shop will open early. We want to lure in a few Christmas shoppers and—"

"You have to eat dinner," Kellan said.

"I know." Sometimes it felt as if they were hurtling toward a cliff, unable to stop themselves from falling completely and utterly in love. It was one thing to spend time with Nan and Jordan and his brothers. But it was a whole other thing to become friendly with his parents and his sisters.

Expectations were difficult enough to meet, never mind the fact that none of the Quinns knew who she really was. They were just a regular family and she didn't want to do anything to change that. But how long would she have to wait until no one in the world was interested in where she was and who she was sleeping with? Would the press give up after a year? Or would it take longer?

"I'm just all grimy from cleaning up the shop and I'm tired and I don't think I'd be very good company and—"

Kellan pressed a finger to her lips. "No worries," he

said. "You don't have to come. I don't want to pressure you to—"

"No!" Gelsey cried. "It's not that, it's just—"

"You're right," he said. "There's no reason for you to spend time with my family."

Gelsey bit her bottom lip, knowing that whatever she said next wouldn't come out right. She'd fallen into this relationship so quickly and so easily and never thought about the repercussions. She'd taken advantage of Kellan, used him for a place to escape, and now she'd become a part of his life. "Maybe it's too soon for all this?"

His fingers tangled in her hair and he gently turned her face up until she looked into his eyes. "I'll go have dinner and I'll meet you back at the cottage later." Kellan brushed his lips against hers. "Maybe we'll bring in the tub and make you a nice bath. Right in front of the hearth."

"That would be nice," Gelsey said.

A frown worried his brow and he studied her shrewdly. "Are you all right?"

"I'm fine," Gelsey said. "Just a bit tired."

"We should get some sleep tonight," Kellan murmured. "We have been keeping rather late hours, considering you're a working woman now. You'll need your rest if you're going to get this place in shape." He bent closer and kissed her again, drawing his tongue along the crease of her lips. And then, as if he couldn't resist, he pulled her against him and deepened his kiss, his tongue invading her mouth, desperate to taste and possess.

When he was through, Gelsey was left breathless, her mind spinning. It was so easy to get caught up in the desire and the way their bodies melded so perfectly. But she and Kellan had been living in a fantasy that was slowly being unraveled by reality.

Kellan pressed his palms to her temples and smoothed her tangled hair away from her face. Then he kissed each eyelid, the tip of her nose and her mouth. "You do look tired. I'll eat quick and bring you something from the pub. We'll have a lazy night at home."

Home, Gelsey mused. Is that what they had together? Had they made a home? Did he think of her as part of that home or was she still just a visitor? "That sounds nice. I'll see you in a little while."

She walked him to the door then gave him a quick kiss before he left. Sighing softly, Gelsey flipped the sign in the front window to Closed and pulled down the shade on the door. This was real life now. She couldn't hide from it. And either she'd make a mess of it, or she'd carve out a place for herself.

And somewhere along the way, she'd figure out exactly how she felt about Kellan Quinn.

KELLAN STOOD in front of the hearth, staring into the glow of burning peat. With a soft curse, he glanced at his watch for only the fourth or fifth time in the last few minutes. He'd returned from the pub to find the cottage dark and empty. Assuming that Gelsey had been delayed at the shop, he'd hauled the tub in from the pantry next to the kitchen and filled it with a hose from the kitchen sink.

But after an hour of waiting, the water was cold and the fire was dying. Kellan strode to the door and pulled it open, staring down the road that led from the village into the hills above town. The Fiat was gone, so she wouldn't be walking back. He paused. Unless she wasn't able to get it started.

The first thing on his list of things to do would be find a more dependable car for her to drive. Kellan grabbed his jacket and headed for his own car. He'd drive to the shop and fetch her, before she completely exhausted herself. Since she'd begun, Maeve had decided to make a quick visit to her sister's place, leaving Gelsey with long hours and no days off.

It took just a few minutes to drive into the village, but when he rapped on the shop door, it went unanswered. The Closed sign was hanging in the window and from what he could tell, all the lights were off.

Kellan tried the pub next, thinking that Gelsey may have changed her mind and they might have just missed each other. But when he walked in, his family was still gathered at the tables they'd pushed together, finishing up their dinner as the pub began to fill with the Friday-night crowd.

"Hey, you're back," Danny called from behind the bar. "Did you bring Gelsey?"

"She's not here?" Kellan asked.

"No. I thought you said she'd decided to go home after work."

Kellan leaned on the edge of the bar. "I was up at the cottage and she wasn't there. Is she with Nan or Jordan?"

Danny cocked his head toward the kitchen. "They're still here. They're in the kitchen getting Lily's birthday cake ready." Danny motioned Kellan to follow him to the end of the bar. "I'm glad you came back. I have something I have to show you."

"I really don't have time," Kellan said. "I need to go find—"

"It won't take but a minute. Jaysus, Kell, your woman can certainly survive on her own. Don't be so possessive. It's not good for a relationship."

"What are you, a feckin' psychiatrist?"

"I'm just statin' a fact," Danny said.

"Why don't you tell me your meaning so that we don't have to waste breath figuring it out."

"You're lookin' like a man desperately in love."

Kellan shook his head, fixing his brother with a dismissive glare. "And you're full of shite, you are."

"I don't know," Danny said. "You're getting yourself all bothered about a girl that you've been sleeping with for a couple weeks, all worried when she isn't where she's supposed to be."

"We have an understanding," Kellan said. "Neither one of us is planning our future together."

"Hey, maybe you should be. I know I'm going to

marry Jordan. If I were you, I wouldn't let a girl like Gelsey get away, if you catch my meaning."

"This is none of your business," Kellan said. "Hell, I'm not going to lie. I like having her around. We get along great. We're very…compatible. But we're a long way from spending our lives together."

"Hey, we're all just trying to help you out here," Danny said. "You could at least be grateful. We're all doin' our part to get her to hang around."

"What the hell are you talking about, brother?" Kellan leaned forward and grabbed his brother's arm. "Explain yourself."

Danny cursed beneath his breath and shook his head. "Nan and Jordan think she's just grand. They're helping her dust out that shop. And Markus and his committee are determined to get her to buy it from Maeve." He drew a ragged breath. "Perhaps you might want to make an effort on your end. I mean, it's clear to me that you're in love with her. I see the way you look at her. It's the same way Riley looks at Nan and I look at Jordan. No use denying it, Kell."

"So you and the rest of the town have my whole life planned out for me?"

"No," Danny said. "Well, maybe a bit. But you've got to take it from here, mate."

Kellan stood up and pressed his hands along the edge of the bar. "Why don't you all just bugger off and leave me to my own life."

"So you are in love with her, then," Danny said.

A long silence grew between them. He wanted to

admit that his brother was right, but Kellan had always expected that love would be a concrete concept, that he'd never have any doubts once he found it. He was in love with the Gelsey he knew, the woman who curled into his naked body at night, the woman who could merely glance his way and make him burn.

"I'll take that as a yes," Danny said.

"So, what am I supposed to do about this? She might as well be a mermaid for all I really know about her."

"And if she has some horrible past? Would that make a difference? Would it make you want to walk away?"

"No. As far as I'm concerned, we began the day I found her on the beach." He paused, wondering if he ought to reveal more. "Or maybe we began years ago."

"How is that?" Danny asked.

Kellan braced his elbows on the bar and leaned in, lowering his voice to a whisper. "Do you remember that day when we were lads and we found that box buried in the sand at Smuggler's Cove?"

"Why are we whispering?" Danny whispered back.

"Remember the girl? The one who buried it?"

"There was a girl?"

"Yeah. She ran off and we chased her. I caught up with her and she kissed me. That was the first time I ever kissed a girl."

"What does this have to do with Gelsey?"

"That was her," Kellan said. "At least I think it was. I can picture that girl in my mind and Gelsey is just an older version."

"Have you asked her about this?"

Kellan shook his head. "No. Because if it was her then this thing between us becomes something very different." He scowled at Danny's puzzled look. "Don't you get it? It's destiny."

"Oh. Like Jordan and me. And Nan and Riley." Danny glanced both ways, then reached into his pocket and pulled out a small box. He pried open the top to reveal a diamond ring. "I'm going to give it to her for Christmas," he whispered.

Kellan stared at the ring. "It's grand. She's going to love it."

"Get things settled with this girl," Danny warned, "or you might lose her."

Kellan pushed away from the bar and turned for the door. He'd like nothing more than to get things settled between them. But Kellan didn't have a clue how Gelsey felt about a future together. She obviously planned to stay near Ballykirk, at least for a while. But did her plans include him? Somehow, Kellan knew it would be impossible to get a straight answer from her on that subject.

He jogged back to his car and got inside, then turned toward the cottage. There was one thing he had to check before continuing his search. As he drove up the hill, Kellan decided there was only one other place she might have gone—back to Winterhill.

She'd acted strangely distant when he'd stopped by the shop, been preoccupied with something other than business. And she was usually so happy to get out and socialize.

He pulled up in front of the cottage, then jumped out of the car, leaving it running. Throwing back the front door, Kellan called her name, but there was no answer. He headed directly for the bedroom, then opened the wardrobe and dug into the clothes inside.

He found the green dress exactly where he'd put it the night they met. It was still flecked with sand and bits of seaweed. Clutching the wrinkled fabric in his fists, Kellan chided himself for even considering the possibility. She wasn't a mermaid and she wouldn't leave him to return to the sea.

"Winterhill," he murmured.

The sun was already sinking beneath the western horizon as he drove along the coast road, through Derreeny. On the far side of the village of Curryglass, he turned onto a narrow country lane and followed it as it wound between two dry stone walls.

The lights from the house were visible from the road. He swung the car into the driveway and breathed a sigh of relief when he saw the Fiat parked in front of the house. As he got out of the car, Kellan realized that he'd need an explanation for how he knew where she was. Though she'd mentioned Winterhill in her answers to his five questions, she hadn't given him directions.

He strode up to the front door and grabbed the cast-iron knocker, but the door swung open before he could signal his presence. The gray-haired woman he and Danny had met earlier smiled warmly up at him as she wiped her hands on her apron. "Hello," she said. "You've come back."

"Yes," Kellan said. "I—I'm here for Gelsey. I'm—her friend."

An eyebrow rose slightly and she regarded him with a suspicious eye. "You're Kellan."

He nodded. "Yes, I am. She's mentioned me?"

"Once or twice, in passing." She held out her hand. "I'm Caroline. I'm the housekeeper. We've met before. You were the young man with the camera, the other day."

"I was. She's here?"

"She is. But I'm afraid she's sleeping. She stopped by to pick up some old Christmas decorations for the shop and when I went upstairs to check on her, she was curled up on her bed, sound asleep."

"May I go up and see her?" Kellan asked.

"I suppose it wouldn't hurt. You two haven't been arguing, have you?"

Kellan shook his head. "No. Everything is fine. She's just been working very hard lately and I'm a wee bit worried."

Caroline stepped aside and allowed him to pass. "Top of the stairs, second door on the left."

He took the stairs two at a time and found her room. The door was ajar and he silently pushed it open. Gelsey was curled up on the bed, still in her shoes and socks and the clothes she'd been wearing at the shop. Kellan carefully sat down on the edge of the bed, but she didn't stir.

Holding his breath, he pulled the down-filled duvet up from the foot of the bed and stretched out beside her.

Kellan watched her sleep for a long time, wondering at the life she'd lived before him. From what he knew of it, it hadn't been particularly happy.

He could give her more than what she'd had. He could make her happy. Unable to help himself, Kellan leaned forward and touched his lips to hers. The contact startled her and she opened her eyes, staring at him incomprehensibly. "Hello," he murmured.

Gelsey frowned, pinching her eyes shut and then opening them again. "Is it you?"

"Yes," Kellan said.

"What are you doing here? How did you find me?"

"I followed you here the other day. I guess I got a little impatient and couldn't help myself. Does it make a difference?"

"No," she said softly.

"Can I stay here with you tonight?"

She nodded then reached out and touched his face. "I don't want to fall in love with you. But sometimes you make it impossible not to."

"I know exactly what you mean," Kellan said. He captured her mouth in a long, deep kiss.

Slowly, they tugged at clothes, undressing each other beneath the duvet. He curled up behind her, his mouth pressed against her nape, and a moment later, he was buried in her warmth. Kellan moved slowly, enjoying the sensations that pulsed through his body with every lazy stroke.

He skimmed his hands over her hips and along her belly, then found the spot between her legs, damp with her desire. He touched her there, gently caressing her until her breath quickened and her body arched against him.

They reached their release together this time, with barely a sound between them and when it was over, he wrapped his arms around her and waited until she fell asleep, the two of them still joined.

He'd fallen in love with her. Danny was right and there was no denying it. But how had it happened? They'd only known each other two weeks. Or maybe they'd known each other since that summer day he'd chased her across the meadow.

There was only one thing that Kellan was sure of. He intended to keep Gelsey in his bed and in his life for as long as she'd have him. If he was lucky, that would be a very, very long time.

# 7

THE DARK PANELING in the conservatory was draped with fresh greenery, holly and pine mixed with red twigs, putting Gelsey in a cheery mood. Caroline had laid out a sumptuous breakfast on the small table and Gelsey poured herself a cup of hot chocolate, wrapping her hands around the bone-china cup. "Try the scones," she said, reaching for her favorite, a candied-cherry scone. "They're still warm."

Kellan sat across from her, his hair sticking up in spikes, a sleepy look in his eyes. He took a sip of his coffee and smiled. "I like this."

"What? Being waited on hand and foot?"

"No. Sitting here with you, reading the newspaper, watching the rain come down outside, thinking about Christmas."

They'd both fallen asleep sometime around eight the previous night and slept soundly until seven the next morning. Since it was Saturday, Gelsey didn't need to be at the shop until noon, so a leisurely breakfast was exactly what she needed.

"I can't believe how well I slept," she said, breaking off a bit of scone and slathering it with butter.

"I know. Me, too. I guess we really should try to get to bed early at least one night a week."

"You think so?" She pushed the plate of scones in his direction. "Try one. I used to live on these when I was younger. Caroline used to send me boxes of them at boarding school, although they never taste really good unless they're right from the oven."

"So this is where you spent your summers?" He nodded approvingly. "It's a beautiful house, Gels. Classic country architecture. It's the kind of house everyone wants these days but it's impossible to replicate."

"It is nice. Whenever I think of home, this is the place I think of. Even though my parents never lived here."

"I grew up in the cottage."

"Our cottage?" she asked.

Kellan nodded. "Yeah. The seven of us in that tiny little cottage. It seems impossible when I think back on it, but it was fun. After we all left home, my folks moved to one of the flats above the pub."

"How long have you been here? I mean, this visit?"

"I've been here for about three months. I was staying with a friend in Portugal. We were in Rome for a few days, then back to Portugal. And then I came here."

"And you left Portugal for the damp and rainy west coast of Ireland?"

"Yes," she said. "It was time to leave and I wanted to spend the holidays at Winterhill."

"So you have a house and you're going to own a business soon. I guess that means you're planning to hang around county Cork for a bit longer?"

Gelsey nodded. "That's the plan for now."

He bit into a scone. "Good. I like that."

Gelsey reached for the salver in the center of the table, loaded with all the dishes in a traditional Irish breakfast. She filled a plate for Kellan and set it in front of him. "Here. Eat. You're going to need your strength."

"Why is that? Are we going back to bed after we're finished eating?"

"No. You're going to help me out at the shop today. I have some heavy lifting to do."

The wood fire in the small hearth popped and snapped, creating a relaxing counterpoint to their conversation. Gelsey was glad he'd come to Winterhill. He needed to know what her life had been as a child in order to understand how it had gone so badly off track as a young adult. It wasn't an excuse for her behavior, simply a point of reference.

A knock at the front door echoed through the quiet interior of the house and Gelsey frowned. "Who could that be?"

A few seconds later, Caroline came hurrying in. Her face was pale and her hands were twisted tightly in the front of her apron. "Oh, dear," she muttered. "I'm afraid I've made a terrible mistake."

"What is it?"

"At the door. He called yesterday and I told him you weren't home and that I hadn't seen you for days. He said he'd call every day until he had a chance to speak to you."

"Antonio?" Gelsey asked, her stomach twisting into a knot at the mention of his name.

"Who's Antonio?" Kellan asked, his mouth full of buttered scone.

"Tell him I'm not here," she said. "Send him away. I don't want to see him or talk to him. It's finished. And if he wants his ring back, he can find it at the bottom of the Atlantic just off…" She turned to Kellan. "What's that place called again?"

"Smuggler's Cove?"

"Yeah," Gelsey said. "Smuggler's Cove."

"All right," Caroline said. "But how should I explain the extra cars in the driveway?"

Kellan pushed his chair back from the table. "Go back to the kitchen. I'll take care of this."

A voice echoed through the house. "Gigi! I know you are here. This is childish. We have to talk."

Gelsey shot up out of her chair. "You will not. Sit down." She pointed to his chair. "Sit!" She neatly folded her linen napkin and dropped it next to her plate. "I'll take care of this."

In truth, she should have done this months ago. Rather than running away from him, she should have explained why she was leaving and how it was impossible for her to continue with such a destructive relationship.

It was his fault she was in trouble with the Italian police. He'd started the argument with the photographers and she was only trying to defend herself. Unfortunately, she'd been the one to break the photographer's nose, not Antonio.

Though Antonio could be stubborn at times, he was smart enough to see that they weren't right for each other. But she'd played games with him in the past, taunting him with threats of leaving just to get him to behave himself. Now that she'd finally done it, it was no wonder that he didn't believe it was real.

"I'll be right back," Gelsey said. She strode through the dining room and into the foyer. As expected, Antonio stood in the doorway, handsome as ever, impatiently tapping his foot and cursing beneath his breath. He froze when he saw her.

*"Dios mio,"* he muttered. "You *are* here."

"I am," Gelsey said, nodding.

He grabbed her arms and pulled her into a kiss, but Gelsey twisted away, holding up her hand in a warning. "Don't do that again."

"Why not? I have missed you, my love. I have been so lonely without you."

"You're going to have to get used to that. I meant what I said on the phone. We're finished, Antonio. You know it, I know it. By now, the rest of the world probably knows it. There's nothing left to talk about."

Gelsey heard footsteps behind her and a moment later, Kellan's arm slipped around her waist. "Is there a problem here?" he asked.

Gelsey looked back and forth between the two men as they sized each other up. Kellan had no idea who he was dealing with. Antonio was known for his quick temper and it didn't take much provocation for him to throw a punch. He'd been sued by at least three photographers for doing just that. "Kellan, I think you should go back to our breakfast."

"Your breakfast?" Antonio shouted. "I see how this is. I am not a fool. This is the man who replaces me, no?"

"Yes," Kellan said.

"No," Gelsey countered. "You were out of my life before I even met him."

"I think it would be best if you left," Kellan said.

"You think I should leave?" Antonio asked. "You think *I* should leave?" He lunged at Kellan, but Kellan quickly stepped aside, shielding Gelsey behind him as he did. Antonio stumbled forward, nearly losing his balance, before he turned around again.

He wasn't expecting the quick jab from Kellan. Blood erupted from his nose and he stopped, holding his hand up to his face, stunned by the turn of events. Kellan quickly handed him the linen napkin he still held and Antonio stuck it under his nose.

"Sorry, mate," Kellan said, his demeanor deceptively calm. "But if you try that again, it will be much worse the second time. Gelsey and I are together now and if I have to beat the shite out of you to make you see that, I don't have a problem doing that at all. So, do you want to fight, then, or will you just be saying your goodbyes and go on your merry way?"

Antonio's eyes narrowed and he looked at Gelsey. "You will want me back," he said. "You forget, you need me. Without me, your whole life falls apart. Are you willing to risk that, Gigi? It would be a terrible mistake. A year of your life is a terrible thing to lose, no?" He walked through the door and slammed it shut behind him.

Gelsey and Kellan stood next to each other, silently watching the door, Gelsey's heart slamming in her chest. Well, at least she had her answer. Unless she made nice with Antonio, he had no intention of testifying on her behalf. She heard a car start and then it roared off down the driveway. She released a tightly held breath. "I suppose that could have gone worse," she murmured.

"Will there be any more of those types coming around?" Kellan asked.

"No," Gelsey said.

"Good. Not really the way I like to start my day." He frowned. "What did he mean about a mistake? What about a year of your life?"

"It's nothing," she said. "Old arguments." Gelsey drew a ragged breath and closed her eyes. Why not tell him? At least he'd understand her reluctance to commit to staying in Ballykirk. If the trial didn't go her way, she could spend some time sitting in an Italian jail.

The tabloids were all hoping for that. Not a month or a year, but at least a few weeks so they might get some good photos of the "criminal" going in and coming out. Gigi Woodson in jail would sell a lot of papers.

They walked back to their breakfast and she sat down across from him, watching as he finished his scone.

"What would you do if I had to go back to Europe for a while?" Gelsey asked.

He looked up. "For what? To see him?"

Gelsey shook her head. "Just to tie up some loose ends. Would you forget all about me?" She held her breath, waiting for his answer. Kellan wasn't the kind of man who'd wait forever and he'd already grown impatient with her refusal to consider their future together.

She couldn't imagine wanting a man more than she wanted him and there were times when a future with him seemed like the perfect way to spend a lifetime. Would her old life always come back to haunt her? Could she really start over again? Was "normal" was even possible for Gelsey Woodson?

"I don't know. How long would you be gone?"

"Not long," she said.

"I suppose I'd miss you. But then, I could always come with. When are you planning to leave?"

Gelsey pushed out of her chair and circled the table, then crawled onto his lap, wrapping her arms around his neck. "Never," she whispered. "I want to stay here forever." She snuggled against him, pressing her face into the curve of his neck.

"I'd like that," he said.

She sighed and hugged him tighter. For now, she'd

ignore the dark cloud looming on the horizon. If she wished it hard enough, maybe it would just dissolve before it ever reached her. Or perhaps, by the time it moved overhead, she'd know exactly what to do. She kissed his cheek. "You're pretty good with your fists," she said.

Kellan held up his right hand. "Fist. If I would have used them both, the guy would be headed for hospital right now."

IT HAD TAKEN HIM the entire afternoon, but the cottage looked perfect. Kellan smiled to himself as he went around the room and lit the candles he'd bought. A big bouquet of flowers sat in the middle of the table and he'd brought out the old copper tub and placed it in front of the fireplace, ready to be filled for a bath.

This was the night, Kellan mused. He and Gelsey were going to determine once and for all what this relationship meant to them. He needed to know if there was a real future with her, because if there was, there were plans to be made.

He glanced over at the table and sighed. He'd been offered the museum job in Brittany and was waiting to sign the contract. He'd also met with some potential investors about a castle renovation near Killarney. A month ago, he would have jumped at the chance to take a job outside Ireland, searching for any excuse for a change. But his life *had* changed and now, he wanted nothing more than to spend all his time near Ballykirk.

Kellan walked into the kitchen and pulled open the

refrigerator to check on the temperature of the champagne. He'd never really done it up proper with a woman before, pulling out all the romantic stops. But there was no doubt in his mind that Gelsey was the girl for him. He wasn't sure how he knew, but he knew, deep down in every corner of his soul, she was the one.

He ought to be surprised at how quickly it happened. Although Riley and Danny had found love at lightning speed, Kellan had dismissed the possibility as a rare occurrence. But now, he'd experienced the same strange phenomenon.

He heard the sound of the Fiat chugging up the hill to the cottage and walked to the door. He opened it and waited as Gelsey pulled the car to a stop at the garden gate. She stumbled out, dragging a canvas bag behind her. The moment she saw him, she stopped and gave him an exhausted smile.

"Long day?" he asked.

She nodded. "Excruciatingly long. Please tell me there's a large glass of wine waiting for me."

"Better than that," Kellan replied, holding out his hand. He drew her inside and closed the door behind her, then helped her out of her jacket.

"What's this?"

"Just a little holiday from all the hard work you've been doing," Kellan explained. "Tonight, I'm going to wait on you hand and foot. I'll make you a bath. I have champagne and candles, and dinner is warming in the oven."

"It all looks so wonder—" she began, before fighting

back a yawn. "Can we just lie down and have a quick nap before we get started?"

"Sure." He took her hand and led her into the bedroom, then sat her down on the edge of the bed. Kneeling, he pulled off her shoes and gently massaged her feet. "How's that?"

"Heaven," she murmured, flopping back on the bed.

He stretched out beside her, lying on his side as he toyed with a strand of her hair. "Can I get you anything?"

"A kiss would be nice," she said, turning to face him. Gelsey pointed to her bottom lip. "Right here. This is the only place on my body that isn't utterly exhausted."

Kellan leaned forward and gently nibbled at her lower lip. A long sigh escaped her body and he wove his fingers through her hair and kissed her again, this time more purposefully.

"Oh, that's much better," she said, smiling. "A girl could get used to this."

"That's what I want to talk to you about," Kellan said.

Her brow wrinkled into a frown. "You look so serious." Gelsey reached out and smoothed her fingers over his forehead.

"I am. But you don't need to look so worried. We've been living together for almost a month now and it's been grand."

"It has."

"And I was talking to Danny the other day and he

plans to ask Jordan to marry him at Christmas and I'm reckoning we ought to make some plans ourselves."

"Plans?"

"Yeah. Maybe it's time we…formalize things between us."

She pushed up on her elbow, her frown deepening. "Formalize? What does that mean?"

"Make a commitment to each other."

"How would that change anything?" Gelsey asked.

Kellan was confused by her comeback and at first, didn't have an answer. "I—I guess it wouldn't. But I have to make some plans with my work and I—"

"What kind of plans?"

"I've got to make a decision on the job in France. It would take me out of Ireland for a long time. You'd be here. I'd be there."

"Do you want to take the job?"

"I don't know," Kellan said. "I don't want to leave you."

"How would your decision change then?"

"I guess I wouldn't leave you."

"See. That wasn't so difficult. We don't need to decide anything right now. We'll just do what we feel."

Kellan sat up and shook his head. "No. I don't want to turn this job down and then have you run back to Europe. That's not the way it's supposed to go."

"You know exactly how it's supposed to go?" Gelsey asked. She sat up beside him and folded her hands in her lap. "Tell me. I'd like to know, too. I've been trying to figure it out for the past ten years and haven't gotten it right yet."

He could hear the sarcasm in her voice and for a moment, he thought better of continuing the conversation. But this was a matter that they needed to resolve. "There's just a certain progression that most people follow. Like…Riley and Nan and Danny and Jordan. They've decided that they want to spend the rest of their lives together and—and everyone knows it."

"So a public announcement will make it all work out for us?"

Kellan cursed beneath his breath. Was she deliberately trying to start an argument? The last thing he wanted to do was fight with her. She was tired and tended to get a bit irrational when she didn't have enough sleep.

"We should probably discuss this later," he dodged. "After you've had a kip. Why don't you crawl under the covers and I'll let you sleep for a bit."

She shook her head. "I think we should get this settled."

"No," Kellan said. "You're in no mood to talk."

"I'm in the perfect mood." Gelsey stood up and began to pace back and forth. "Let me see. I've been engaged three times in the past seven years. Married once."

Kellan gasped. What the hell? This was definitely not going the way he'd planned. "You've been married?"

"Yes. To someone who was already married, so

it wasn't legal. I was twenty-three and very stupid. I thought I was in love, but I was proven wrong. I thought I loved them all and in the end it didn't mean anything."

"Why haven't you told me this?"

"Because it's in the past," Gelsey said. "And I wanted to start fresh. But I can't do that if I keep making the same mistakes over and over again."

Kellan grabbed her hand to stop her pacing. "All right. We're done. This isn't the right time or the—"

"No. We should get this straight. I don't want you to plan your life around me, Kellan. I want you to do what makes you happy. And if that means going to France to work on a project then that's what you need to do." She shrugged. "I'm not sure I'll even be here. If I am, when you come home, we'll take up where we left off."

"And in between? We just forget about each other?"

"No, of course not. You know I care about you."

"But you don't love me."

"That has nothing to do with this conversation. You're talking about commitment. I can love you without making a commitment to you, can't I?"

"Yes," he said. "Of course, but—"

"No buts." Drawing a deep breath, she turned and straddled his legs, then sat down on his lap. Wrapping her arms around his neck, she kissed him, her mouth trailing from his lips to his ear. "I'm happy now. I don't want anything to change."

She tipped her head as she stared into his eyes. But his anger must have been evident in his gaze, because she suddenly stood up. "But then, maybe it would be good to have some time apart."

Kellan gasped, stunned by the turn in the conversation. He stood also, catching her off balance. Gelsey stumbled back and he caught her arm. "How did we get from that to this? We love each other but we should spend some time apart?"

Gelsey nodded. "I think I'm going to spend the night at Winterhill. You can think about what you want to do and I won't be here to…distract you."

"I don't think that's a good idea," Kellan countered.

"Sure it is. Besides, I have some business I need to take care of tomorrow morning at the house, so I won't have to get up early and drive over there."

"Why do I get the feeling that I just turned everything arseways between us?"

"You didn't," Gelsey said. "Nothing has changed."

Kellan didn't believe her. In truth, he could see the confusion in her eyes, the frantic way she kept avoiding his gaze. Hell, she'd been engaged three times? This was a woman who was pathologically frightened of commitment and here he was, pushing her to declare her feelings and plan a future with him after they'd only known each other less than a month.

Jaysus, could he be much more of a gack? How had his brothers managed to find mates when all he could do was stumble around and blather on about his plans and his needs. "If you want to go, that's fine," he finally said. "I'll stop by the shop tomorrow. Maybe we can have lunch?"

"Yes," Gelsey said. "Lunch would be perfect." She kissed him quickly, then slipped into her shoes. Reaching out, she placed her palm on his cheek. "Don't look so worried. Everything will be fine."

As she walked out of the room, Kellan sat down on the edge of the bed. Raking his fingers through his hair, he cursed. This was not the way it was supposed to go. He'd finally found a woman he could love and he'd made a complete mess of it.

He heard the car start and walked to the window. Watching through the lace curtains, Kellan willed her to come back inside, to forget everything that he'd said to her. But instead, she drove off down the hill toward the village and the coast road to Winterhill.

Kellan wandered out into the great room. He felt as if he'd just gone ten rounds in a feckin' boxing ring. His head hurt and he couldn't put a coherent thought together. "I need a drink," he muttered.

Grabbing his jacket, he opened the front door and stepped out into the evening chill. There was plenty to drink down at the Speckled Hound. And maybe his brothers might be able to explain exactly where he'd gone wrong, because he sure as hell couldn't figure it all out.

"Danny said you've moved out of the cottage."

"Where did he hear that?" Gelsey asked.

Jordan shrugged. "I think Kellan told him. He stopped by the pub a few nights ago and got really pissed. Danny had to drive him home."

Gelsey picked at a piece of lace on Nan's wedding dress, smoothing it down until it lay perfectly on her shoulder. "I didn't exactly move out. Some of my things are still there. I'm just staying at my place for a while until we sort out our...issues."

They'd gathered at Danny and Jordan's cottage behind the blacksmith's shop to look at the dress that had just arrived from a bridal shop in Cork. To Gelsey's eyes, it was the perfect dress for the perfect bride. Nan had chosen a simple fitted sheath, bare at the neck with handmade Irish lace covering her arms and shoulders. It hugged the curves of her body, flaring out at the knees, making the dress both sexy and conventional at the same time.

Jordan groaned. "No, you can't have issues. We don't want you to have issues." She paused. "What are your issues?"

"It's nothing serious, really," Gelsey said. "He just wants everything to be...official. Written in stone. And I'm just not sure I can do that. Every time I've tried that in the past, it's blown up in my face."

"Antonio?" Nan asked.

Gelsey blinked in surprise.

"Kellan told Danny who told Riley. He thinks you're going to go back to him."

"Danny?" Gelsey asked.

"No, Kellan. He thinks you're going to go back to Europe and to Antonio."

Gelsey stepped away from Nan then took in the sight of her new friend, dressed in the gown she'd be married in. "You look beautiful." Tears pressed at the corners of her eyes. How had it been so easy for Nan and Jordan to surrender to love? And why did she find it so impossible? Surely, they'd made mistakes in the past. How could they be so certain it was the right thing to do?

If Kellan truly loved her, then he'd have to accept her the way she was, with all the baggage that came along. And if she had to spend some time in an Italian jail, then he'd be there for her when she got out. And he'd be there for her every day for the rest of her life.

It took so much courage to put her life, her future happiness, in his hands. At this moment, she felt as if she could get out without mortal wounds. But if she went on much longer, leaving him would destroy her.

"I'm sorry," she murmured, brushing a tear from her cheek. "I don't know why I'm so…silly." Her voice wavered. "I'm usually not so emotional."

"It's all right," Nan said. "You don't have to hide it with us. So, he knows about your life in Europe? The tabloids?"

Gelsey shook her head. "We haven't really discussed it."

"And what about the thing with the photographer?" Jordan asked.

Gelsey gasped. "You know about that?"

Jordan nodded. "You mentioned it that time we talked. Nan saw it in *Hello!*"

"Yeah, well, it's the truth. I have to go right back into that mess with the photographers and the reporters and all the people who want to examine my life with a microscope. Nobody knows me here and it's been wonderful."

"We know you," Nan said. "And Kellan knows you. And everyone who knows you cares about you. We don't care about that other stuff."

"I haven't told Kellan about court," Gelsey said. "I just know everything is going to change once I go back. All the magazines will have pictures and I don't want him to get caught up in that. He doesn't deserve that."

Jordan slipped her arm around Gelsey's shoulders. "I think you should tell him. He would want to know."

Gelsey forced a smile. They were right. She didn't want to keep him in the dark any longer. Kellan would understand and he would see why she couldn't make any commitments until after the last part of her past was dealt with.

"Can we just get back to your wedding plans?" Gelsey said, reaching out to grab Nan's veil. "You need to put this on. Are you going to wear your hair up or down?"

Nan stared at her reflection in the mirror. "What do you think?"

"Down," Gelsey said. Jordan seconded her choice. "But maybe with a bit of curl?"

Nan nodded. "I always expected that I'd be a bag of nerves before my wedding day, but I feel strangely calm."

"You do?" Jordan said. "How can that be? I get nervous just looking at you."

"I know I'm doing exactly the right thing," Nan said, a serene expression on her face. "I have no doubts. I was meant to marry Riley, the same way you're meant to marry Danny."

"He hasn't officially asked me yet," Jordan said. "But I suspect there's a proposal coming soon. He's been acting weird lately. Staring at me all the time with this dopey smile on his face." She shook her head and turned to Gelsey. "And then comes you and Kellan."

"We'll see about that," Gelsey said. "It's just not going to be as simple for us."

"Do you love him?" Nan asked.

"I think I do. I tell myself I do, but I've never said it out loud. But then, I've fallen in love so many times, I'm not sure I really know how I'm supposed to feel. I guess I'm just waiting."

"For what?" Jordan asked.

"I'm not sure. Maybe a sign? Or a moment of clarity? I don't know what it is, but there has to be something that will make me sure of my feelings. Something that I never felt before with the others."

Nan and Jordan both turned to look at her, shared concern evident in their gazes. But Gelsey waved them off. "Don't look at me like that!"

"Well, we've been ordered to bring you along to the pub," Jordan said. "We're all going to have dinner there and then go into Cork to catch a late movie. A triple date."

"Does Kellan know about this?"

"Of course he does. He said he's barely seen you this past week."

"We were supposed to have lunch on Monday, but he had to cancel. He said he needed to spend some time in Dublin before the holiday." In truth, Gelsey wanted to see Kellan. Over the past few days she'd been left to wonder whether his feelings for her had cooled.

He called her a few times at the shop, just to check in, but his tone had been distant and his mood unreadable. She needed to look into his eyes, to hold his hand, to kiss him again if only to reassure herself that he still loved her.

Nan turned back to the mirror. "All right. I'm going to have to take this dress off, even though I adore looking at myself."

Jordan adjusted the veil. "You do look beautiful."

"Wait!" Gelsey cried. "I have something for you. I can't believe I almost forgot!" She grabbed her bag and rummaged around in it until she found the flat velvet box. "I know you need something borrowed and if you like these, then I want you to wear them on your wedding day."

Nan took the box from Gelsey's outstretched hand and slowly opened the top. Her breath stalled in her throat as she caught sight of the ruby necklace and matching earrings.

"I know you're using red in your bouquet and I thought this might go. You don't have to wear them if you don't like them."

"No!" Nan cried. "They're beautiful. Where did you get them?"

"My grandmother left me a lot of beautiful jewelry and I've never thought to wear any of it. I sat down and looked at it the other day and thought this would be perfect for you."

Nan pulled Gelsey into a fierce hug. "Thank you. Gosh, I feel like royalty now."

Gelsey helped her put the necklace and earrings on, then nodded. "I thought so. They do look lovely."

"Jordan!"

The sound of Danny's voice echoed through the quiet cottage. "We're in here," Jordan called from the bedroom.

A moment later, Danny appeared in the door, breathless, his hair windblown. "Gelsey, there's a guy in town who's been looking for you. I think he's a photographer. He's been hanging around asking questions. Kellan sent me over here to get you."

"Oh, dear," Nan murmured.

"I guess my past has just caught up with my present." Gelsey was resigned. "I think it would be best if I got out of town as quickly as possible."

"Kellan is waiting for you behind the pub. He told me to bring you to him. He'll get you out of town."

Gelsey picked up her jacket and purse, then gave Nan and Jordan a hug before she hurried to the door. "I'll see you both soon. Thanks for inviting me."

When they got outside, she and Danny walked along the back side of the cottage and the smithy, through an alleyway behind the bakery, and then over a low fence to the small garden behind the pub. Kellan was waiting there, his back braced against the side of the building.

"You're back," Gelsey said as he took her hand.

"Just," he murmured. "Lucky thing."

"Where is he?"

"Out front. Riley has been keeping him occupied. Although, he did manage to get a fair bit of information from Maeve, before she realized what he was doing in town."

"How did he know I was here?"

"I suspect Antonio sent him. The guy probably started asking questions in Curryglass and worked his way down the coast. He's got pictures he's showing everyone."

"I'm sorry," Gelsey said.

"For what?"

"They're not going to leave me alone. Now that Antonio's talking, it makes the story even better. I'm sure he's giving them all sorts of juicy details."

"What kind of details does he have to give?"

"The kind that sell papers," Gelsey replied. "There are some things I haven't told you, but I really want to. First, though, we need to figure out how we are going to get out of here."

"We aren't," he said. Kellan pointed to a stairway that led up to the second floor above the pub. "Riley has a flat next to my parents' place. He'll come and tell us when the guy leaves and then we can leave."

"Where are we going to go? He'll find me whether I'm at Winterhill or here."

"He can't be everywhere at once. And everyone in town knows to send him in the wrong direction. After a few days, he'll be so mixed up, he won't know which way to turn."

"Or he'll call in a bunch of his friends," Gelsey said. "They rarely travel alone. It's always in packs."

He started up the stairs in front of her, holding her hand as they climbed. "Why do they even bother? You're not living that life anymore, not that I really know anything about that life." He turned to face her. "I don't care, you know. We all make mistakes and then we move on."

"My mistakes will follow me around forever," she said.

When they reached the landing, Kellan opened the door and stepped aside. Gelsey walked into the kitchen of the small flat. It wasn't at all what she expected for Riley's bachelor flat, then she realized that Nan was living there with him. She heard the door click shut behind her.

In an instant, his hands were on her waist, spinning her to face him and picking her up at the same time. Kellan wrapped her legs around his hips and set her on the edge of the kitchen table.

"Wait," she murmured. "We need to talk."

"I don't care what you have to tell me," Kellan said. "I don't need to know. It doesn't change this."

Gelsey held tight as his mouth came down on hers in

a desperate kiss. All the doubts and insecurities she'd felt over the past few days dissolved and she surrendered to the pleasure that raced through her body at his touch.

She reached for the buttons of his shirt, needing to touch warm skin and hard muscle. Her lips trailed her fingers as she tugged the shirt from the waist of his jeans. Frustrated by her pace, Kellan shrugged out of his jacket, then tore the shirt off his body and tossed it aside.

A long breath slipped out of her body as she ran her hands over his naked chest. It had been only a few days, but it was as if she were parched with thirst for the sight of him, the scent of him, the taste of his tongue in her mouth.

He slipped his hands beneath the hem of her skirt, sliding it up along her thighs as he stepped between her legs. Her fingers trembled as she worked on the button fly on his jeans.

"God, I missed you," he murmured as Gelsey skimmed his jeans down over his hips.

Grabbing her legs, he pulled her against his body and a heartbeat later, he was inside her. Gelsey moaned softly as he began to move, her body falling into a familiar rhythm. How had she ever done without this? Every nerve in her body cried out for his touch, and the ache deep inside her was suddenly soothed with each stroke.

This man was all she ever needed and everything she'd ever wanted. Yet she couldn't bring herself to believe that the feelings between them could last. This desire could…but desire was a very different thing than love.

# 8

A SMALL CROWD WAS GATHERED on the main street of Ballykirk as Kellan drove into town. "What the hell is going on here?"

Danny peered through the windscreen. "I don't know. Isn't that Maeve's shop?"

Kellan had left Gelsey asleep in the cottage that morning while he and Danny drove to Bantry to pick up supplies for the pub. They'd had a late night, having waited until nearly midnight before leaving the flat above the pub and sneaking back up the hill to the cottage.

Rosie Perry, the owner of the only bed-and-breakfast in Ballykirk, had passed along a message that the photographer had taken a room and was planning to stay for at least another day or two. She'd promised to call Kellan with any news of his movements.

Kellan reached into his pocket for his mobile, then cursed beneath his breath as he noticed the battery levels were dead. "Can you see what's going on?"

"There's the photographer," Danny said. "And it looks like Gelsey is there along with Dealy, Markus and Johnnie. Maeve's there, too."

Kellan pulled the car up to the curb and hopped out, closing the distance between him and the crowd in a few long steps. Strangely, Gelsey didn't seem to be in any distress. She was smiling for the crowd as she spoke.

"Maybe you can get a photo of Maeve and I under the sign." She pointed above her head and the photographer reluctantly focused on the pair of them and clicked his shutter.

"What about you and Antonio?" he said.

"Oh, that's old news. Now, let me tell you about our new product line. It's all natural, made from a special kind of kelp harvested off the coast of the Aran Islands. Here, get a photo of this jar. Isn't it beautiful? Mrs. Logan has tried the facial scrub." She drew Ardelle Logan out of the crowd. "Tell this nice gentleman what you thought."

Ardelle Logan held the jar up for the photographer, smiling as she spoke. "It made my skin so wonderfully soft. It doesn't smell very pretty, but it works."

"Perhaps we can get a photo with our tourism committee too," Gelsey suggested.

"Do you have any plans to return to Europe, Gigi? Maybe to see Antonio? Is it true that he came here looking to take you back?"

"Oh, no. I'm happy right here. Helping Maeve turn this shop into everything that it can be. Would you like to come inside? I'd love to show you around. Wait, maybe we should get a few more photos outside."

"And what about the charges that are still pending against you? There's been talk that after the criminal trial, the guy is going to sue you."

The crowd around her went silent and Kellan glanced over at Danny. "Charges?"

"I—I'm sure that I'll be cleared of any wrongdoing," Gelsey said.

"And what if you're not?" the photographer asked.

Kellan pushed through the crowd to Gelsey's side. "Listen, I think you got what you came here for. It's time to leave, mate."

"Who are you? Are you and Gigi together? Does Antonio know about this, Gigi?"

Kellan grabbed his arm and pulled him along through the crowd. "She doesn't want you here. Leave her alone."

The photographer wrenched out of his grasp and began to snap pictures of Kellan. But within seconds, most of the men in the crowd surrounded them both, moving in on the photographer.

He held up his camera. "All right, all right. I get the message." He hoisted it over his shoulder, then nervously walked through the crowd. "She's turned into a crashing bore anyway. She was much more fun when she was drunk." He turned back and looked at Kellan. "You're not Quinn, are you?"

Kellan shook his head. "Rooney is the name. I run the petrol station near the docks. You're welcome to come down and take a few snaps of my place." He slipped his arm around Danny. "This is my brother. He helps out."

"Do you know Kellan Quinn?"

"Oh, he doesn't live here. He lives in Dublin," Dealy said.

"That's what I've been told," the photographer replied.

"I'm sure he's in the book," Markus added. "K-E-double L-A-N. Ring him and he'll probably let you take his picture, too."

"Either you're all crazy or you're acting like you are," the photographer said. Kellan watched as he strode down the street to his car, got inside and headed out of town.

The crowd slowly dispersed, chatting amongst themselves about the possibility of being on the cover of *Hello!* or the *Tattler*. They didn't seem to care about the bomb the photographer had just dropped. What kind of trouble was she in? And why would it require a trial?

Before long, Gelsey was the only one standing in front of the shop. "I'm going to take the car down to the pub," Danny said.

"Great. I'll meet you there in a few minutes." Kellan stepped up to Gelsey, then looked over his shoulder to make sure there weren't any other photographers lurking about. "Are you all right?"

She nodded. "He'll be back. Don't think he believed that story you told him. They're much smarter than that. He'll pay someone for more information and he'll catch a photo of us together and he'll have his picture and story to sell."

"What story? We're not doing anything wrong."

"Gigi Woodson hiding out in Irish village with new boy toy. Do you really want to be known around the world as my boy toy?"

Kellan chuckled softly, then leaned close to drop a kiss on her lips. "I don't know. Do I?"

"Definitely not," she replied.

"So, now that you're the biggest celebrity in town, I suppose you're not going to want to go out to lunch with me, are you?"

Gelsey shook her head. "Maybe we should—"

"Why not?"

"I just think we ought to—"

"But I'm really hungry."

Gelsey reached into the pocket of her skirt and pulled out an envelope, waving it in front of her face. "All right. My paycheck. Maeve gave it to me this morning. I'm pretty sure it should buy us lunch."

"Where are you going to take me?" he asked.

"There's only one place in town that serves lunch. It's called the Speckled Hound. You ever been there?"

"I don't believe I have," Kellan said, playing along. "Lead on."

She slipped her hand into his and they walked down the street. "How was your trip to Dublin?" she asked.

"Good," he said. "Everything went well. It's another job, this time just outside Waterford."

"What about the job in France?"

"We're still considering that," Kellan said. "It's a big commitment and I'm not sure Jordan wants to spend that much time away from Danny."

"Right," she murmured. "I guess she wouldn't."

"And what about you?" Kellan asked, turning to face Gelsey and pulling her to a stop. "I understand you have a little problem with the law in Italy?"

Gelsey stopped short. "Now you want to talk about that?"

"Do you?"

"Do you want the long story or the short?"

"Short," he said.

"I accidentally hit a photographer and broke his nose. He's filed assault charges. Antonio is my only witness. The hearing for the case is scheduled for January. If I don't win, I might have to go to jail—for a little while." She drew a deep breath and let it out. "There. That wasn't so bad."

"Is this why you've been so reluctant to talk about the future?"

Gelsey shrugged. "In part. There are some other things that we probably should talk about. Stupid things that I've done. I just didn't want you to think less of me. And sooner or later, someone is going to tell you these things or you're going to read about them and maybe you won't like me as much anymore."

"Well, I don't think that will happen. But it might help if we didn't have to sleep in separate beds. Hell, in separate houses. Why are we doing that?"

"I guess I'm wondering that, too," Gelsey said. "But

it's different now. Before, I was staying with you because I was running away from my old life. Now I have a new life and I have to figure out how I want that life to be."

"What do you need to figure out, Gels? It's not that difficult."

"All right. Where do we live? You have a place in Dublin, we can't live there. The cottage belongs to your parents, we can't stay there forever. I have a house, we could live there, but I'm not quite sure I'm ready for that."

"I see your point," Kellan said. "But we can spend a few nights a week at your house and a few at the cottage until we decide what to do."

He pulled open the door to the pub and they walked inside. Gelsey saw Danny behind the bar and smiled at him, but Kellan led her to a booth on the far wall, a spot that offered them the maximum amount of privacy.

Sitting down across from her, he grabbed her hand and brought it to his lips. Their gazes met and for a moment, Kellan saw the fears vanish from her gaze. He was making progress in the right direction. Very slow—but positive—progress.

"Maybe we ought to start dating," Kellan suggested. "Forget about the sex and the sleeping together. We never really started at the beginning. Maybe that's the problem."

"What are we going to do around Ballykirk that we haven't already done?" Gelsey asked.

"There are plenty of things to do. We can sit down

at the harbor and watch the fishing boats come it. We can walk to the library and look at the new books. The greengrocer teaches a cooking class every other Wednesday night. And there's always Tuesday-night bingo at St. Margaret's."

"Bingo sounds lovely," Gelsey said. "And I'll drive. Now that I have my own car, I can pick you up."

"You're driving a forty-year-old Bentley. That thing should be in a museum, not on the road. Do you know how much that car is worth?"

"No. It was my grandmother's. She loved that car. It was just sitting in the carriage house, so I thought I'd drive it."

"And then there's Nan and Riley's wedding. I don't have a date for that and I was hoping you'd agree to come with me."

Gelsey smiled, then twisted her fingers through his. "I suppose I could be convinced. I don't have any other plans for New Year's Eve."

"That would be a rare one for me," Kellan said. "I never have a date for New Years."

Danny appeared at their table, a pad and pen in his hands. "I'd assume the two of you are here for lunch? We have a lovely shepherd's pie, bangers and boxty, and salmon patties with chips. And the regular sandwiches and salads."

"Shepherd's pie," Kellan said. "And a half pint of Guinness."

"Same for me but water," Gelsey said.

After Danny had gone to put in their orders, Kellan asked, "How has work been?"

Gelsey pulled his hand toward her. "Good. Well, maybe not good, but it's improving. We've had a lot of new customers come in. After this morning, I'm sure we'll have more."

"That's good."

"There's going to be all sorts of talk, Kellan. It doesn't bother me, but I don't want you to get caught up in it."

"It'll be good for business. Have you thought any-more about buying the place from Maeve?"

"I have. But it's a little difficult to make plans with everything hanging over me."

"Then don't let it bother you. Go ahead and make plans. Buy the shop. And if things don't go well in Italy, then figure that out when you have to."

"I suppose I could do that," she murmured.

They chatted about the shop until Danny brought their food. As Kellan watched Gelsey dig into her shep-herd's pie, he nodded. "I think we should call this our first date."

"Why is that?"

"Because a girl like you probably doesn't kiss on the first date. I'm thinking I might get lucky on our second."

"You had all the luck you could handle the night we met," Gelsey teased. "I'm going to take things much more slowly this time around." He felt her bare foot slowly creep up the inside of his calf until she rubbed his thigh.

Kellan grabbed her ankle and placed her foot squarely in his crotch. "I can see you're the kind of girl my mother warned me about." He rubbed her foot over the front of his jeans. "It's a rare pleasure to meet you, Gelsey Woodson."

CHRISTMAS WAS ONLY two days away and Maeve Dunphrey's Potions and Lotions was experiencing what could only be considered a holiday rush. They'd had customers waiting that morning when Gelsey opened and there had been a steady flow of people in and out of the shop, picking up late gifts for friends and relatives.

Gelsey had picked up some colorful wrapping paper and ribbon in Bantry and for the last week had been wrapping every purchase that left the store. To her surprise, customers were stopping in to buy just because of the free gift wrapping.

She had hoped to find a moment to talk to Maeve. After a lot of thought and a few phone calls to her banker, she'd decided to make an offer on the shop. Kellan had been right. She needed to think beyond what would happen in January and this was an opportunity she couldn't pass up.

She had a life here in Ballykirk. She had friends, a man who loved her, people who were happy to see her each day. And even after the entire town found out who she really was, it didn't matter. They still treated her like the girl Kellan saved from the sea.

She hadn't told Kellan about her decision yet. She'd become superstitious since the arrival of the photographer, just waiting for the other shoe to drop. But now she felt confident that no matter what happened, this was exactly where she belonged.

"I haven't see the shop like this in, well, it's been years," Maeve exclaimed. "I bless the day I hired you, Gelsey. Look what you've done. It's a miracle."

"The shop just needed a bit of modernizing," Gelsey said as she arranged a display of natural sponges in a wicker basket. "I'd like to sit down and talk with you after the holidays. I'd like to make an offer to buy the shop. I'll give you a fair price. Enough for you and your sister to take ten cruises around the world."

Maeve picked up a pot of beeswax lip balm and slowly turned it over in her hand. "About that," she said. "I—I'm not so sure I want to sell anymore."

Her words hit Gelsey like a slap in the face. "What? I don't understand."

"Well, everything is going so well. We've had so many new customers stop in and the shop has never looked better. And I've never really gotten on with my sister. She's bossy and stubborn and she spends far too much time in front of the telly. We'd never be able to live together."

"But, I thought—"

"I know. And I am sorry, dear. This is just so much fun now and I don't want to give it up. You understand, don't you?"

Gelsey felt the frustration bubbling inside her. *She*

was the reason the shop was doing well, *she* brought the customers in, *she* gave them what they wanted. Without her, Maeve would have still been digging herself out from beneath dusty boxes of ten-year-old product.

"I'd still love you to work here," Maeve continued. "The customers adore you. And of course, we'd renegotiate your pay. But, if you want my advice, dear, you're much too clever to stay in this small town. You should be running your own place in London or Paris."

Gelsey opened her mouth, ready to argue her point, but then she snapped it shut. "I'm going to take my break now," she said, trying to keep her voice calm and her manner indifferent. It wouldn't do to burn any bridges right now. Perhaps Maeve could be persuaded to change her mind.

Maeve glanced at her watch. "Go right ahead. I think I can handle things. And when you come back we'll discuss that raise."

Gelsey grabbed her coat and pulled it on over the cashmere sweater and skirt she'd chosen that morning, then retrieved her purse from behind the counter. She couldn't get out of the shop fast enough, but when she reached the safety of the street, she didn't curse or scream. Instead, tears erupted from the corners of her eyes and there was nothing she could do to stop them.

She headed toward the pub. Her immediate reaction was to find Kellan and tell him what had happened. But as she walked, Gelsey realized that this wasn't his problem, it was hers. She'd been the one to naively put all her efforts into improving the shop. She'd been the one to spend her own money on gift bags and wrapping paper and real grosgrain ribbon for the boxes.

She'd dusted and mopped and toted and carried until every muscle in her body ached and she'd been rewarded with happy customers and increased sales. Maeve was right—she was clever. And she did know what she was doing.

Gelsey wiped away her tears. Why was she crying? She didn't need the job. She had plenty of money left in her trust find.

She walked past the pub and down to the waterfront. The smell of the sea was thick in the damp air. She sat down on a bench that overlooked the harbor, fixing her gaze on a fishing boat that was chugging out of port.

People went to work every day and some of them worked at jobs they barely liked. But she'd wanted to find something to make her life meaningful, something that made her proud of what she did with her day. She'd wasted so much time, and now that she'd finally decided on a future for herself, it had been snatched away from her before she'd even begun.

The tears started again and Gelsey didn't try to stop them. She was alone. And the emotional release was the only reaction she could muster. But when she saw Dealy Carmichael and the rest of the Unholy Trinity approaching, Gelsey quickly composed herself and pasted a smile on her face.

"Good morning, lass," Markus called. "What are you doing out here on a chilly day like today?"

"Just admiring the view," Gelsey said, forcing a cheerful tone into her words.

"We're working on a shopping brochure for the town," Dealy said. "We'll be sure to add your shop to the map."

"Good. I'm sure Maeve will appreciate that."

They continued past her, fishing poles in hand. Once they were out of sight, Gelsey drew a ragged breath. Closing her eyes, she tipped her head back and tried to relax.

How had she managed to fool herself yet again? She'd convinced herself that she could live happily ever after in Ballykirk. But she should have known that nothing ever worked out in her favor.

Another sob rocked her body and she covered her face with her hands, her cheeks already growing wet with tears.

"Gelsey?"

The sound of Kellan's voice startled her and she sat up and wiped her face with her palms. "Hi. Sorry, I was just resting my eyes."

"The boys told me you were down here," he said, sitting down next to her. "What are you doing? Aren't you supposed to be at work?"

"No."

"But it's the Friday before Christmas."

"Just go away," Gelsey said. "Leave me alone."

He reached out to pull her closer, but she fought his embrace, moving to the other end of the bench.

"Would you like to tell me what this is about?"

"Maeve doesn't want to sell the shop anymore. Now that it's doing so well, she's decided to stick around. Of course, she wants me to continue working there. With a lovely raise."

"That's good," Kellan said.

"I don't want to be taking orders from Maeve for the rest of my life. She knows that I'm responsible for all the new business, but it's still her shop. I guess I've done my job too well."

"I'm sure that's true," Kellan said. "Maeve may be a big crazy, but she's not blind. She'd be lucky to have you."

"I'm not going back there. I don't want to work for Maeve. She's a lovely woman, but I need to do something for myself."

"Gelsey, I know you haven't had a job in the past, so you might be a bit naive about how things work in the real world. This happens all the time. Employees are taken advantage of, are underappreciated and overworked. That's just the way the world operates." He finally got hold of her hand and this time Gelsey didn't pull away. "My first job, I was amazing. I did brilliant work. But my boss took it all and passed it off as his own. In the end, his boss found out, he was sacked and I moved up into his spot. I had a choice and I decided to stay. But you can do anything you want."

Gelsey laughed. "You say that as if it's the easiest thing in the world to do. I liked Maeve's shop. I knew I could make a success of that."

"So, open up your own shop."

"Selling what? I don't think Ballykirk can support two shops selling kelp facial masks and sea-salt scrubs."

"Gelsey, if you're going to let this stop you, then you aren't cut out to run a business."

Gelsey snatched her hand away. "Whose side are you on?"

"This isn't about sides. It's about business. You can do anything you want. You just have to decide to do it."

"I did decide and it blew up in my face."

"I think you're being a bit dramatic," Kellan said.

Gelsey stood, her tears now replaced with anger. She'd at least thought that Kellan would understand, but he seemed to be taking Maeve's part, which only added to her anger. "I have to go. I don't want to talk about this anymore and I don't want to talk to you."

"Come on, Gels. Don't get mad. This isn't a big deal. You pick yourself up and you move on."

"No? It's a big deal to me. A really big deal. And if you don't understand that, then you don't understand me."

"You're mad at me?" Kellan asked. "Just because I disagree with the way you're handling this?"

Gelsey walked by him and started back toward the shop. "Don't even think about following me," she shouted.

To her relief, Kellan didn't. She managed to make it to the Bentley without having to talk to anyone. Gelsey tossed her purse inside, then got behind the wheel and started the car. The mechanic she'd hired to look at it had encouraged her to get it tuned up before driving it, but she hadn't had time.

The engine sputtered at first, refusing to start, but after the sixth try, it roared to life. She put the car in gear, made a wide U-turn on the street in front of the shop and headed out of town.

He was right. She'd just have to find another opportunity, a better chance to make a future for herself. But would that be in Ballykirk? And would it be with Kellan?

Gelsey scolded herself. She shouldn't have reacted the way she had. He was only trying to help. But Kellan knew what he wanted from life. It had always been easy for him. Since she'd come back to Ireland, she'd been living in a strange kind of limbo, waiting for everything to make sense.

"I don't need him," she murmured to herself as she steered the car along the coast road. "I can take care of myself."

"HERE IT IS," Kellan said. "What do you think?"

Jordan stared at the facade of the shop, nestled between the Ballykirk post office and Roddy Murphy's Sporting Emporium, a confused expression on her face. "About what?"

"The possibilities," he said. He pulled a key out of his pocket and pushed it into the lock on the front door, then stepped aside so Jordan could enter.

"Are you going to bid on the renovations? Who is this for?"

"A friend," Kellan said.

Jordan sucked in a sharp breath as she caught sight of the cluttered interior. Everywhere they looked, old appliances were stacked and scattered, some in pieces. "Is this for Gelsey?"

Kellan nodded. "Yeah. You probably heard about what happened with Maeve. Gelsey quit her job there after Maeve decided she didn't want to sell the shop."

"I know. Nan told me. It happened yesterday and it's all around town. People are plenty angry with Maeve, but she seems as happy as a clam with all her new business. Is Gelsey even interested in staying in Ballykirk now?"

"She was before," Kellan said. "And I hope she hasn't changed her mind. I'm going to do everything I can to give her a reason to stay."

"You're going to buy her this shop?"

"No. She's going to buy the shop. I'm going to renovate it for her." Kellan stood in the center of the huge ground floor. Up until a few months ago, it had housed Eddie Farrell's appliance-repair shop. Eddie had heard about Maeve's change of heart and had come rushing over to the pub last night with an offer of his own. "What do you think?"

Jordan walked along one wall lined with shelves that were filled with old toasters. "I don't know what to think. It's hard to see past the junk."

"Eddie Farrell is ready to sell. And he won't be changing his mind. He's offered to include his inventory, but I'm not sure it's worth keeping."

"It would take a lot of work," Jordan said. "Much more than Maeve's place. But look at these shelves. They're original. And these cases are beautiful."

"I know. That's why I need your help. We're going to need to find more display cases and shelving units and tables. I know you've been all over Ireland looking for furniture for Castle Cnoc. I'm hoping you can find what we need to make this place work."

"I already know of a few places to check." Jordan grinned. "This is going to be a fun project. So what is she going to sell?"

"I don't know," Kellan said. "She'll have to figure that out. But at least whatever she sells will be here in Ballykirk." He turned to face Jordan. "Do you think you could make some sketches? Maybe choose some paint colors and put together some boards. I want to set something up so that when I bring Gelsey here, she'll be able to see the potential."

"Today?"

"No. I was hoping to show it to her on New Year's Eve. After the wedding. I want to get some of this junk cleared out first."

"That would be perfect," Jordan cried. "Wow, you are a romantic, aren't you."

He couldn't help but laugh. The notion was so absurd, but he'd spent a lot of time considering what approach would best appeal to Gelsey. "I'm learning."

"Every woman appreciates romance," Jordan said, patting him on the arm. "Even a good attempt is appreciated. When Danny and I were living at Castle Cnoc, he used to bring my coffee up to the bedroom in the morning so I could wake up slowly. All those little gestures add up and one day, it just hits you square in the face. Oh, my God, I'm in love with this man."

"That's the way it went?"

"I really knew it when we were dancing naked in the rain," she said.

"Danny?"

She nodded. "Don't you ever tell him I told you that." Jordan went silent for a moment and then giggled. "He looked so sexy."

Kellan thought about the night Gelsey had sent him out in the rain. She'd stood in the door and watched him, her eyes alight with amusement. Would she remember that moment in the same way?

"Will Gelsey be coming for Christmas Eve tonight?" Jordan asked.

"I haven't talked to her since yesterday. I decided I ought to give her a chance to cool off. But I'm going to drop her Christmas present at Winterhill later this afternoon. Hopefully, she won't slam the door in my face."

"Why would she do that?"

"Because, in addition to being a romantic, I can sometimes be a Bombay shitehawk."

"And what exactly is that?"

"An arse of the first order," Kellan replied. "I didn't really handle the situation very well yesterday. She didn't take kindly to my suggestions. And I guess I don't blame her. She has plenty of money, so she doesn't have to keep a job for the wages."

"You better take more than a gift over there," Jordan warned. "You better have a full-blown apology ready." She glanced around once more, then nodded. "Have you taken measurements?"

"I have," Kellan said. "I'll text them to your mobile."

"And I'll get to work on the boards. I can probably have them done in three or four days, unless it gets too crazy before the wedding." She pushed up on her toes and kissed Kellan's cheek. "Dinner is at seven, gifts at nine and Midnight Mass after that. Don't be late. Your mother has been working all week on this."

"I won't. I'm going to head over to Winterhill right now. I'll be back in plenty of time."

Kellan wandered through the shop once more, making mental calculations of the cost for renovation. Though Maeve had an existing business, it might appeal to Gelsey to build something from the ground up. He walked to the rear of the shop and looked through the window in the door. An old stone building that used to serve as a carriage house stood close enough to connect the two. If Gelsey wanted to make a product, he'd design a beautiful workroom for her, too.

But as Kellan walked back through the shop to the front door, he realized that before he could sell Gelsey on staying in Ballykirk, he'd have to convince her of his feelings for her. There was one gift that could do the trick, one thing that he had in his possession that would prove they were meant to be together.

Winter had arrived in southwest Ireland. Rain was coming down in sheets and it was almost cold enough for snow. A white Christmas was a rarity in county Cork, but Kellan never stopped hoping.

He jumped in the car and headed for the pub. His mother would have wrapping paper and ribbon, something he couldn't find at the cottage. She also made the best fruitcake. It probably wouldn't hurt to take a loaf along for Gelsey's housekeeper, Caroline.

The wind blew in behind him and Kellan shook the water out of his hair as he stood at the door. Christmas Eve was always celebrated in the large room at the pub. The door was closed to the regular patrons at three in the afternoon and Maggie Quinn took over, arranging gifts under the tree, setting the long string of tables for dinner and finishing the last of the meal preparations in the kitchen behind the bar.

"Hey, Ma."

"Oh, you're here. Come help me with these tables. Every one of them wobbles. I swear, I'm tempted to toss them all out on the curb and have your father order new."

"You could just buy a few long tables to use for the holidays," Kellan suggested. "I've got a few in my office in Dublin that we use for blueprints."

"I'll put that on my list for next year."

Kellan helped her shove folded cardboard beneath the wobbly legs and when they'd made a table long enough for eighteen, he watched as she laid the table linens over them all, turning the scarred pub furniture into an elegant dining table.

"Look what Jordan found," Maggie said, holding up a length of red fabric. "Chair covers. They'll make the table even more beautiful. And a table runner. She has such good taste, that girl. Not that Nan doesn't. She's picked out music for us tonight." Maggie glanced over at Kellan. "And what about Gelsey? Will she be joining us?"

Kellan shook his head. "No. I don't think so."

"There's plenty of room at the table."

"I know. But we're taking a bit of a holiday from each other. I'm going to drive over to Winterhill and drop off her gift. I'll invite her, but I wouldn't plan on her coming."

Maggie paused. "Is everything well with you, then?" she asked.

Kellan nodded. "Yeah. I love her, Ma. She's really something. And you'll love her, too."

Maggie reached out and placed her palm on his cheek. "If you love her, Kellan, I know I will. Just follow your heart and you'll never go wrong."

"Thanks, Ma," he murmured. "Now I have to steal some paper and ribbon. I have to wrap her gift."

"Upstairs on the kitchen table. Take the silver foil and the gold ribbon. And one of those little gold glitter bells to make it pretty. What are you going to give her?"

"Something that I've been holding on to for a very long time."

# 9

GELSEY SAT IN THE DARKENED ROOM, staring into the flickering fire. Nearby, an elaborately decorated Christmas tree twinkled with tiny white lights. Everything was exactly as she remembered it, the house smelling of freshly baked gingerbread and pine boughs.

She'd driven to Cork to shop that morning, picking up presents for Caroline, Nan and Jordan. They lay wrapped beneath the tree. She'd struggled with a present for Kellan, unable to decide on anything suitable. She'd looked at expensive watches and interesting books, designer clothes and antique fountain pens, but nothing seemed right.

It might have helped if she knew where she stood with him. But since their argument the day before, Gelsey had been too embarrassed to call him. And he'd obviously been too angry to call her. Things had been so perfect between them and now everything had fallen apart.

She pressed her palm to her heart, aware of the ache

that had settled there. Over and over, she'd questioned her feelings for him, but now, faced with a life all alone, she'd come to realize that she was in love with Kellan.

Her days and nights meant something when she was with him. She wasn't just racing through life, she was actually living it, breathing it all in and savoring each moment. She'd tried to think about her time with Antonio and not one second could be marked as memorable. But every moment with Kellan had been etched into her mind, a vivid picture of perfect happiness.

Last Christmas had been spent on a beach in Thailand, drunk on champagne after Antonio had presented her with a diamond engagement ring, the same ring she'd thrown into the sea. Everything in her life had changed and yet, she didn't regret a single decision she'd made.

She took a sip of her wine, then stretched her stocking feet out to the warmth of the fire. She picked up her magazine and flipped through the article on Irish linens. Since yesterday, she'd been racking her mind trying to come up with an alternate plan for a shop, but everything she thought of just didn't seem to excite her. Irish linens, rare books, designer fashions, Gaelic art, hand-crafted jewelry... She had lots of ideas, but no passion for any of them.

Her mind wandered to thoughts of Kellan. That's where her passion focused. She could imagine the Quinn-family Christmas, laughing and teasing, everyone in a boisterous mood. Gifts spilling out from under a tree, endless plates of food. She'd never had a Christmas like that, with boundless happiness. The holidays had always brought tension between her parents, before and after the divorce.

But this Christmas would be a fresh start. From here, she'd begin to build a life for herself. And if it couldn't be in Ballykirk, then she'd find another spot, maybe Bantry or Glengarriff. This next year was going to be even more exciting than the past month had been.

"I'll get that," Caroline called, poking her head in the room.

Gelsey looked away from the fire. "What?"

"The door," Caroline said. "There's someone at the door."

"Oh," Gelsey said. "Fine." A pair of photographers had camped out on the road in front of the gate, waiting for her to come out, but she didn't plan to give them the satisfaction. Maybe one of them had decided to venture up to the door. "If it's a photographer, call the garda."

Caroline disappeared and Gelsey went back to her contemplation of the fire—and of Christmases past. A smile touched her lips. "Deck the halls with boughs of holly, fa la la la la, la la la la." She took another sip of her wine. After dinner, she and Caroline would share dessert and a glass of sherry and then they'd both go to bed. And one more Christmas in her life would be over.

"Gelsey? You have a visitor."

Gelsey twisted around. "A visitor?"

"It's Kellan. He's brought a gift. He'd like to see you. Can I show him in?"

She hesitated. "Sure. Tell him to come in."

She got to her feet, the wineglass still clutched in her hand, and sat on the arm of the sofa. When he appeared in the doorway, her breath caught in her throat and she had to remind herself to take another. "Hi."

"Hi," he murmured. "I hope I'm not disturbing—"

"No, I was just sitting here having—"

"It's Christmas Eve and—"

"Would you like a glass of wine?" Gelsey jumped up to fetch him a drink from the small table against the wall. When she'd filled the glass, she held it out to him. "Sit. The fire is warm. It's so damp outside. Your hair is wet."

"Are we actually talking about the weather?" Kellan asked.

"I hope not." She sat down on the sofa and he took a spot next to her.

"I'm sorry about yesterday. I should have been more supportive."

"No," Gelsey said. "I was acting like a spoiled brat. You were right. I don't know anything about having a job. These things happen all the time. I need to learn to adjust my plans."

"It's caused a bit of a stir around town," he said. "I spoke to Dealy this morning and he and the rest of the tourism committee are very concerned. The only one in town who seems happy about your leaving is Maeve."

"Well, I'm glad that I could help her out. Maybe she'll keep some of the changes I made."

"Have you decided what you're going to do?"

Gelsey shrugged. "I'm going to take my time and explore all my options."

"Would one of those options be spending the rest of your life with me?"

Reaching out, she took his hand in hers. "I do love you, Kellan. I'm certain of that. But—"

He put his finger over her lips. "No buts," he said. "Let me just let that first part sink in for a few moments." He closed his eyes, a smile of pleasure curling the corners of her mouth. "Yeah, that was nice. You love me."

"I do," she said from behind his finger. Gently she pulled his hand away. "But I've got to take some time to get to know myself."

"We could do that together," Kellan said. "I hardly know you. We could kill two birds with one stone."

Gelsey laughed. "I suppose you're right. But I'm not sure you're ready for the person I might be. I've done a lot of really idiotic things in my life and living a true and real life is probably going to be difficult. I'm going to get frustrated and impatient and I know I'm going to say stupid things."

"Gelsey, I love you exactly the way you are. I wouldn't have you change a thing. And if you can put up with me, then I can certainly put up with you."

"I'm just not sure I'm ready for a relationship yet," she said. "I don't think I've ever *not* been in a relationship. I've just moved from one man to another. I broke my engagement to Antonio one night and met you the next morning."

"So, if we aren't together, maybe we could just be friends. You don't have a lot of friends around here, except for Nan and Jordan. We could spend time together, maybe have dinner a few times a week and—"

"I thought you might take a project in France," she said.

"I decided against that," he replied. "I'm going to be sticking close to home for a while."

"Is that because of me?" she asked.

"No, it's because of me. I'm doing it for purely selfish reasons. And I've got a job in Ballykirk that will keep me busy for a while." He glanced down at the gift he held. "I brought you something. A Christmas gift. Even if we are just friends, I wanted you to have this." He nodded. "Go ahead, open it."

Gelsey neatly pulled away the silver paper to reveal the old biscuit tin she'd buried on the beach. She smoothed her hand over the dented top, the illustration faded by time. "I gave this to you the first time we met," she said. "I buried it in the sand hoping you would find it."

"Me?"

"I used to watch you and your brothers from the top of the cliff and I thought you were the most beautiful boy in the entire world. I was madly and hopelessly in love with you."

"Have you known it was me this whole time?"

"I think I did. But I found the box in the bedside table, and then I knew for sure." Gelsey glanced up, tears clouding her vision. "You were the first boy I ever kissed."

"You were the first girl I ever kissed. And I was in love with you, too. I went back to the cove every time I could, hoping you'd be there again. But you never came back."

Gelsey slipped her fingers through his, her gaze fixing on their hands locked together. "Thank you for bringing it back."

"There's something inside," he said. "Besides your treasures. Open it up."

She pulled off the lid and recognized all the contents except for one thing. Gelsey pulled out the key and held it up. "What is this for? The cottage?"

Kellan shook his head. "No. It's for your future. If you decide to stay here, to make a life here, then that key will open up an interesting opportunity."

"What is it?" she asked.

"You'll just have to come to Ballykirk and find out for yourself."

"I'm coming for Nan and Riley's wedding," she said. "Before that, I'm going to New York to see my mother. My father will be there, too. He has some meetings in Washington after the first of the year."

"You are coming back," Kellan said.

She nodded. "Yeah. I'm just going to be gone a few days."

Kellan slowly stood. Gelsey wanted to pull him back down, to stay with her for the rest of the evening. But she knew he had places to be. Christmas with the family and church after that. "Thank you for coming," she said. "I'm sorry I didn't have a gift for you."

"But you did." He pointed to her face. "That smile. I'm going to enjoy that for weeks. And you said you love me. That's better than a lump of coal in a guy's stocking. I guess I'll see you at the wedding then," he said.

"I'll walk you to the door." Gelsey slipped her arm through his and they slowly strolled out into the foyer. She wanted to lead him right up the stairs and into her bedroom. She didn't want him to leave. Yet, she had to force herself to let him go. Making love to him now would only confuse matters.

When they reached the door, he turned to face her. "Happy Christmas, Gels."

"Happy Christmas, Kellan."

They stood there for a long time, just looking into each other's eyes. "Where is the mistletoe when you really need it?" he murmured.

She laughed softly. "I think a Christmas kiss wouldn't do either of us any harm."

With a low sigh, Kellan cupped her face in his hands. Her gaze fixed on his and he bent close and kissed her, lingering over her mouth for a long time before drawing away.

"There. Now the world is right again," he said.

"Please give your family my best wishes," she said.

"I will." He reached for the door, then paused before he opened it. "I love you, Gelsey. I hope you won't forget that."

"And I love you," she said.

He nodded, then opened the door and walked out. Gelsey watched him as he got in the car. Kellan gave her a wave before he drove away. She smiled to herself. It was a beginning, like the kiss they'd shared in the meadow all those years ago.

She glanced down to find that she was still holding the tin in her hand. "My box of dreams," she said. Funny how her dreams had grown so large that a tiny box could never contain them now.

KELLAN STOOD in the front of the church dressed in his best suit and tie. Danny stood beside him in Kellan's second-best suit and tie. Guests had begun to arrive a half hour before the wedding ceremony and he scanned the crowd, searching for Gelsey. She sneaked into church just before the bride started down the aisle, and Kellan realized she'd probably been helping Nan and Jordan get ready.

"You can take a breath now," Danny whispered. "She's here."

"Yeah," Kellan said. "All right. So things are definitely looking up."

As the organ began to play the processional, the three brothers walked to the railing and waited there for Jordan and the bride. Riley and Nan had planned a simple ceremony, but they'd spent time decorating the church with vivid red poinsettias, fragrant pine garlands and hundreds of candles.

Nan looked beautiful, but Kellan's full attention was

focused at the rear of the church, on Gelsey. She wore a fashionable hat and pretty green coat, almost the color of the dress she'd been wearing the morning he found her on the beach.

When Nan took Riley's hand, Kellan was forced to turn around, but not before talking one last look. She smiled at him and gave him a little wave and Kellan sent a silent thanks to the heavens. She'd shown up and she was smiling at him. Things were going quite well.

Throughout the ceremony, Kellan was tempted to glance back at her, anxious for another look. Although the focus of the guests should have been on Riley and Nan, Kellan got the impression that there were just as many people wondering about the state of the relationship between him and Gelsey. The town of Ballykirk missed their very own celebrity, almost as much as Kellan missed Gelsey's presence in his bed and in his life.

To his relief, the ceremony was short and sweet. Vows were repeated, rings exchanged and before Kellan knew it, Nan and Riley were husband and wife. They walked down the aisle hand in hand, as happy as any two people ever deserved to be. Kellan and Danny followed the couple down the aisle with Jordan walking between them.

"Gelsey is here," Jordan murmured as they walked out of the church.

"I know," Kellan said. "I saw her."

"Everything is ready at the shop. Are you going to take her there now or later?"

"Aren't we supposed to hang about for photos?" he asked.

"We're going to take those back at the pub. Nan and Riley will stay here for a formal portrait."

"What are you two whispering about?" Danny asked.

Kellan frowned at his brother. "Didn't you tell him?"

Jordan shook her head. "He can't keep a secret. He was supposed to wait until Christmas morning to ask me to marry him. He had the whole thing planned and then he asked me the day before, right before we walked over to the pub. Needless to say, I was surprised when he got down on one knee as I was curling my hair."

"It was like the ring was burning a hole in my pocket," Danny commented. "I couldn't wait anymore. I couldn't stop thinking about it."

The moment they got outside, Kellan wandered through the crush of guests, looking for Gelsey. He found her standing near the bottom of the steps, her green wool coat draped over her shoulders. To his surprise, she wore the green mermaid dress beneath it.

"Gels!" he called.

She waved and waited for him to make his way over to her. When he stood beside her, Kellan gave her a quick kiss on the cheek. "Hi. You're here."

"I am. I wouldn't have missed it for the world. Nan looks so beautiful. And Riley. He looks so happy."

"How have you been?"

"Good. My trip to New York was nice. My parents were…well, they were civil to each other. My mother has a boyfriend and she's thinking of getting remarried, which would mean my father would be free of alimony payments, which seemed to put him in a cheerful mood. They didn't get into a screaming match, so I'd say the trip was a success."

"You're staying for the party, aren't you?"

"For a little bit," she said.

He took her hand, then drew it to his lips and kissed the tips of her fingers. "You look beautiful."

"So do you," she said with a smile. "Can I give you a lift back to the pub? I'm parked just down there."

"It's not raining. Why don't we walk. I have something I'd like to show you. Something I need your opinion on."

"What is it?"

"It's right down there," he said.

"Come on, then, let's go."

They strolled silently in the chilly night air, each breath they took clouding in front of their faces. Gelsey looked up at the sky. "I wish it would snow."

"We don't get snow very often."

"I know. But it would be nice just this once. There was snow in New York."

Kellan slipped his arm around her shoulders and pulled her close. "I've never been to New York. Maybe we ought to take a trip there, after your case in Italy has been dismissed."

"How did you know it's going to be dismissed?" she asked.

Kellan stopped short. "It is?"

"We're working out a deal. The photographer is considering dropping the charges in exchange for some exclusive photographs."

"What does that mean, exclusive? Does that mean naked?"

"No! It means…exclusive. He's the only one who gets a chance to shoot."

"Shoot what?"

"Our wedding." This time, Gelsey stopped short, grabbing his arm and turning him to face her. "I know that we haven't really talked about marriage, and I guess that's why I thought it might be an empty promise. And I don't want you to be angry, but I had to offer him something worthwhile. A picture like that could fetch a lot of money." She watched him warily, as if she was waiting for him to explode in anger.

"I think…I think I'm fine with that plan. More than fine. Hell, I don't care if you invite every photographer in the world. I'm just happy that you might marry me someday."

"Someday. Maybe," she said, starting off down the street again. "But don't get your hopes up too high. I might not be the marrying type."

"What does that mean? I might not be the marrying type, either."

When they reached the post office, Gelsey continued to walk, then noticed that Kellan had stopped just one door down. "Right here," he said. "This is it."

Gelsey frowned. "What?"

He reached out and grabbed her hand, then led her

to the front door. The shop was dark inside and Kellan was glad for the element of surprise. When he turned the lights on, he'd know immediately how she felt. "Did you bring the key?"

She nodded. "What is this place?"

"Unlock the door and see for yourself."

Gelsey slipped the key into the lock and turned it, then pushed open the front door. Kellan reached for a light switch and the old fixtures hanging from the ceiling flickered to life.

He heard Gelsey draw in a quick breath and he gave her hand a squeeze. "It's going to take more work than Maeve's shop, but this way, you can do it exactly like you want to." He led her over to Jordan's boards, leaning up against the wall. "You can see a few ideas of what you can do. Jordan drew those."

"You didn't buy this, did you?"

"No, you'll have to take care of that yourself. It's your business and you should own it, although I have negotiated a rather reasonable price for you. I'll take care of the renovations. Jordan can help you decorate. And Dealy says they have some tourism money for advertising. The point is, you have friends here in Ballykirk—good friends. And we all want to help you get your business started."

"I—I don't know what to say," Gelsey murmured. "It's all too much."

"No, it's not. It's exactly what you need. I want you to stay in Ballykirk, I want us to work together on this place and I want you to believe that we have a future together. And when—"

"I do," Gelsey interrupted.

"You—"

"Do," Gelsey said. "I've been thinking a lot over the past week and I do want a future with you. And I don't want to wait. I want that future to start right now. I've wasted too much time already. I know I love you, Kellan. And it isn't some silly fantasy love that I think is going to solve all my problems. It's real and I can feel it deep in my soul. I'm not going to run away from this."

He smiled, relief racing through him until he wanted to shout for joy. He slipped his arms around her waist and picked her up off her feet, kissing her until they were both breathless. "So, I guess my plan worked."

"Your plan? It was my plan," Gelsey teased.

"This? The shop was my plan."

"All right, the shop was your plan. I'll give you that."

"And what do you think you want to sell?" he asked.

"Well, I've been doing a lot of research and I couldn't come up with anything. But then I was walking around Winterhill and I started noticing all the special little things that my grandmother had collected over the years. And I realized that's what I wanted to sell. Beautiful things that make a home warm and cozy. I'll have some antiques. And some Irish linens. Maybe some furniture and crystal. But it will all be Irish. I've been surrounded by all my grandmother's things at Winterhill and I didn't realize how important they were until now."

"I think that's a wonderful idea," he said.

"I had a plan, too," Gelsey said, wrapping her arms around his neck.

"You did?"

She nodded. "The plan started long before you found this place, which is perfect, by the way. The plan started the first time I saw you at the cove, when we were kids. I decided that we were going to spend the rest of our lives together and here we are."

"I guess it's fate then that I found you on that beach. And that I kept that tin box all these years."

"Fate or magic," she said. "Or a bit of both."

"So, if we're going to live together, where will it be?"

"I have a house that's big enough for two," Gelsey said.

"And I have a flat in Dublin, for those times when you need to go in to the city."

"Are we going to live happily ever after?" she asked.

Kellan took her face between his palms and gently kissed her again. "Absolutely. What other possibility would there be?"

"There's always blissfully happily ever after," Gelsey whispered, pulling him into a long and languid kiss.

"Mmm." Kellan drew back. "I think I can make that happen, too."

\* \* \* \* \*

# PASSION

For a spicier, decidedly hotter read—
this is your destination for romance!

## COMING NEXT MONTH
### AVAILABLE DECEMBER 27, 2011

**#657 THE PHOENIX**
*Men Out of Uniform*
**Rhonda Nelson**

**#658 BORN READY**
*Uniformly Hot!*
**Lori Wilde**

**#659 STRAIGHT TO THE HEART**
*Forbidden Fantasies*
**Samantha Hunter**

**#660 SEX, LIES AND MIDNIGHT**
*Undercover Operatives*
**Tawny Weber**

**#661 BORROWING A BACHELOR**
*All the Groom's Men*
**Karen Kendall**

**#662 THE PLAYER'S CLUB: SCOTT**
*The Player's Club*
**Cathy Yardley**

You can find more information on upcoming Harlequin® titles,
free excerpts and more at www.HarlequinInsideRomance.com.

HBCNM1211

# REQUEST YOUR FREE BOOKS!
## 2 FREE NOVELS PLUS 2 FREE GIFTS!

**Harlequin** *Blaze*™

### red-hot reads!

**YES!** Please send me 2 FREE Harlequin® Blaze™ novels and my 2 FREE gifts (gifts are worth about $10). After receiving them, if I don't wish to receive any more books, I can return the shipping statement marked "cancel." If I don't cancel, I will receive 6 brand-new novels every month and be billed just $4.49 per book in the U.S. or $4.96 per book in Canada. That's a saving of at least 14% off the cover price. It's quite a bargain. Shipping and handling is just 50¢ per book in the U.S. and 75¢ per book in Canada.* I understand that accepting the 2 free books and gifts places me under no obligation to buy anything. I can always return a shipment and cancel at any time. Even if I never buy another book, the two free books and gifts are mine to keep forever.

151/351 HDN FEQE

Name _____ (PLEASE PRINT)

Address _____ Apt. #

City _____ State/Prov. _____ Zip/Postal Code

Signature (if under 18, a parent or guardian must sign)

### Mail to the **Reader Service:**
**IN U.S.A.:** P.O. Box 1867, Buffalo, NY 14240-1867
**IN CANADA:** P.O. Box 609, Fort Erie, Ontario L2A 5X3

Not valid for current subscribers to Harlequin Blaze books.

### Want to try two free books from another line?
### Call 1-800-873-8635 or visit www.ReaderService.com.

* Terms and prices subject to change without notice. Prices do not include applicable taxes. Sales tax applicable in N.Y. Canadian residents will be charged applicable taxes. Offer not valid in Quebec. This offer is limited to one order per household. All orders subject to credit approval. Credit or debit balances in a customer's account(s) may be offset by any other outstanding balance owed by or to the customer. Please allow 4 to 6 weeks for delivery. Offer available while quantities last.

**Your Privacy**—The Reader Service is committed to protecting your privacy. Our Privacy Policy is available online at www.ReaderService.com or upon request from the Reader Service.

We make a portion of our mailing list available to reputable third parties that offer products we believe may interest you. If you prefer that we not exchange your name with third parties, or if you wish to clarify or modify your communication preferences, please visit us at www.ReaderService.com/consumerschoice or write to us at Reader Service Preference Service, P.O. Box 9062, Buffalo, NY 14269. Include your complete name and address.

HBI1B

# Harlequin® *Desire*

ALWAYS POWERFUL, PASSIONATE AND PROVOCATIVE.

**USA TODAY BESTSELLING AUTHOR**

# KATHIE DeNOSKY

**BRINGS YOU ANOTHER STORY FROM**

TEXAS CATTLEMAN'S CLUB: THE SHOWDOWN

Childhood rivals Brad Price and Abigail Langley have found themselves once again in competition, this time for President of the Texas Cattleman's Club. But when Brad's plans are interrupted when his baby niece is suddenly placed under his care, he finds himself asking Abigail for help. As Election Day draws near, will Brad still be going after the Presidency or Abigail's heart? Find out in:

# IN BED WITH THE OPPOSITION

*Available December wherever books are sold.*

*Brittany Grayson survived a horrible ordeal at the hands
of a serial killer known as The Professional…
who's after her now?*

*Harlequin® Romantic Suspense presents a new installment
in Carla Cassidy's reader-favorite miniseries,*
LAWMEN OF BLACK ROCK.

*Enjoy a sneak peek of
TOOL BELT DEFENDER.*

*Available January 2012
from Harlequin® Romantic Suspense.*

"**B**rittany?" His voice was deep and pleasant and made
her realize she'd been staring at him openmouthed through
the screen door.

"Yes, I'm Brittany and you must be…" Her mind suddenly went blank.

"Alex. Alex Crawford, Chad's friend. You called him
about a deck?"

As she unlocked the screen, she realized she wasn't
quite ready yet to allow a stranger inside, especially a male
stranger.

"Yes, I did. It's nice to meet you, Alex. Let's walk around
back and I'll show you what I have in mind," she said. She
frowned as she realized there was no car in her driveway.
"Did you walk here?" she asked.

His eyes were a warm blue that stood out against his
tanned face and was complemented by his slightly shaggy
dark hair. "I live three doors up." He pointed up the street to
the Walker home that had been on the market for a while.

"How long have you lived there?"

"I moved in about six weeks ago," he replied as they

walked around the side of the house.

That explained why she didn't know the Walkers had moved out and Mr. Hard Body had moved in. Six weeks ago she'd still been living at her brother Benjamin's house trying to heal from the trauma she'd lived through.

As they reached the backyard she motioned toward the broken brick patio just outside the back door. "What I'd like is a wooden deck big enough to hold a barbecue pit and an umbrella table and, of course, lots of people."

He nodded and pulled a tape measure from his tool belt. "An outdoor entertainment area," he said.

"Exactly," she replied and watched as he began to walk the site. The last thing Brittany had wanted to think about over the past eight months of her life was men. But looking at Alex Crawford definitely gave her a slight flutter of pure feminine pleasure.

*Will Brittany be able to heal in the arms of Alex, her hotter-than-sin handyman...or will a second psychopath silence her forever? Find out in*
*TOOL BELT DEFENDER*
*Available January 2012*
*from Harlequin® Romantic Suspense*
*wherever books are sold.*